THE CASE OF THE
Terrified
Track
Star

THE
NICKI
HOLLAND
MYSTERIES
4

ANGELA ELWELL HUNT

Here's Life Publishers

First Printing, January 1992

Published by
HERE'S LIFE PUBLISHERS, INC.
P. O. Box 1576
San Bernardino, CA 92402

Cover illustration and interior artwork by Doron Ben-Ami
Cover design by David Marty Design

Library of Congress Cataloging-in-Publication Data
Hunt, Angela Elwell, 1957-
    The case of the terrified track star / Angela Elwell Hunt.
        p.   cm.
    Summary: Nicki and her friends try to help their school track team's star runner
Jeremy, who has received a mysterious threat about his next race.
    ISBN 0-89840-338-3
    [1. Track and field — Fiction. 2. Mystery and detective stories.]
I. Title.
PZ7.H9115Cau   1992
[Fic] — dc20   91-32320
                                                         CIP
                                                          AC

For Shane and Roni

Laura **Kim** **Nicki**

Christine   **Meredith**

It's not that I'm madly in love with him or anything, Nicki Holland told herself as she leaned forward to see if Scott Spence was sitting in the bleachers below her. *It's just that he's a good friend and maybe he's out here for the track meet, too.* But Scott was nowhere in the milling group of students in the bleachers.

"Looking for someone?" her friend Christine Kelshaw teased, elbowing Nicki gently. "Who might that be?"

"No one," Nicki said, blushing. "I'm just checking out the track team. Hey, Meredith, you're up on sports. Who's the best guy on our team?"

Meredith Dixon smiled and pointed down at the green field in the center of the track. "We're lucky this year because we've got lots of good guys and girls, too. Jeremy Newkirk grew about six inches since last year, and he's our best distance runner. D. N. Downin is our best sprinter, and Scott Spence is our best high jumper. Elinore Anderson is a good runner, too."

"Scott is on the track team?" Nicki was surprised.

"Yeah. Didn't you know that?"

"No." Nicki was glad she had managed to talk her best friends into coming out for the track meet. Track wasn't exactly the most popular sport at Pine Grove Middle School, but the sun was nice and hot, there was nothing else to do, and she'd been hoping to catch a glimpse of Scott. Now she'd get to see him in action.

A few parents from the PTA were walking through the stands selling popcorn and soft drinks, and Laura Cushman pulled a ten-dollar bill out of her purse and waved it at a man carrying a tray of Cokes. "Five Cokes, please," she said breezily. "For me and my friends."

The girls thanked Laura and passed the Cokes to each other, sipping in silence for a while. Nicki could see the various groups separating on the field: the distance runners, the sprinters, the hurdlers and the long jumpers; guys' and girls' teams of each. Finally she spied Scott's brown hair down at the high jump pit. Now she'd have something *really* interesting to watch.

Kim Park was sitting in front of Nicki, and she turned her head to ask a question: "Why do these people run and jump and throw things out here where it is so hot? Isn't it easier to stay in the gym?"

Laura, the pampered southern belle of the group, answered Kim's question: "You bet it's easier. I've never figured out why anyone would want to come outside and —" she shuddered, " — sweat."

"The gym isn't big enough for these events," Meredith explained. "And the athletes like track because it's a good discipline. Discipline is good for the body and the brain."

"They do it because it's fun," Christine added. "My brother Tommy loves sports, the grungier, the better."

"Maybe they do it because they want to win," Nicki added. "For school pride and all that. I know Coach Linton has wanted to beat Clearwater Middle School since they beat us twice last year. Just because their school is newer and bigger than ours doesn't mean we can't run their socks off!"

"Their socks will come off?" Kim asked, confused.

Nicki laughed. Kim had come from Korea only a few months before, and even though she was a fast learner, some English expressions slid right past her.

"Nicki means we'll run a lot faster than they will," Meredith explained. "But I don't know. Clearwater has a really good team. There was an article on their star distance runner, Aaron Oakman, in yesterday's paper. He's that blond guy down there talking to the Clearwater coach. The article also said the coach is Aaron's stepdad. I wonder what it's like being coached by your dad?"

"Who's our star runner?" Laura asked, straining to see the faces down on the field. "Not that tall skinny kid, I hope?"

"Yes, if you mean Jeremy Newkirk," Meredith said. "He's the kid with brown hair and glasses, number seven. He's my science partner in research class."

"He's in that brainy class with you?" Christine groaned. "Then I bet he won't be able to run. Geeks can't run, Meredith."

Meredith playfully slugged Christine. "Hush your mouth, girl. He's a nice guy. And he's the best runner we have."

"We're doomed, then," Laura said. She lowered her sunglasses and peered out over the top of the lenses. "Just look at the competition. That Aaron Oakman guy is gorgeous. He looks wonderful. He could outrun Jeremy what's-his-name any day."

"Hush, everybody, they're starting the boys' high jump," Nicki said, straining to look across the field where the girls had just finished and the boys were lining up. "It's almost Scott's turn to jump."

Meredith winked at Christine and Kim and they laughed. Everyone knew about Nicki and Scott — they both liked each other but neither would admit anything. "Just friends," they always said.

"Should we cross our fingers for him?" Laura asked, turning to Nicki. "Or do you want us to get his attention so you can blow him a kiss?"

"You do and I'll never speak to you again," Nicki answered, jabbing Laura with her foot. "And crossing your fingers is silly. Either he makes it or he doesn't."

"I don't see how it could hurt," Laura answered, crossing her fingers on both hands.

"Come on, Scott, let 'er rip!" Christine stood and yelled.

Nicki wanted to hide under the bleachers in embarrassment, but Scott either didn't hear or was totally ignoring them. He made it through his first jump without making the bar fall.

"Why do they fall on their backs?" Kim asked.

"It's called the Fosbury Flop," Meredith explained. "In 1968 a guy named Dick Fosbury jumped seven feet four and a quarter inches with that jump. That was two and a half inches higher than the world record, so people have been jumping that way ever since."

"Thank you, Miss Encyclopedia Britannica," Christine teased. "Honestly, Meredith, do you ever turn your brain off?"

"I like to hear Meredith explain things," Kim said simply. "I learn a lot from her."

"You should listen to Meredith more often," Nicki told Christine. "Who knows? You might learn something useful some day."

Christine blew a stray strand of hair out of her eyes. "I doubt it. I'm doing well just trying to get the stuff I'm supposed to learn in school."

"Heads up, Nicki, cutie pie is jumping again," Laura interrupted.

Nicki ignored Laura and held her breath for a second as Scott ran, then jumped up and over the bar. His foot grazed the bar as he fell back, but miraculously, the bar did not fall.

"Whew!" Nicki exhaled in relief. "That was close."

"The runners are lining up down there," Meredith pointed down toward the end of the track. "This is the one-mile race. It will probably come down to a contest between Jeremy Newkirk and that guy from Clearwater, Aaron Oakman."

The starter's gun cracked, and the runners took off around the track. "Go, Panthers!" Christine stood and yelled, but Laura grabbed hold of the bottom of Christine's shirt and pulled her back down on the bleachers.

"You're embarrassing me," Laura said. "Do you hear anyone on the other team yelling?"

"If we had a name like 'Bulldogs,' I wouldn't yell at all," Christine snapped, in a huff. "Where's your school spirit, Laura? I can yell if I want to."

Just then Scott Spence cleared another jump and Nicki stood up to cheer and clap. Meredith jumped up and began yelling for Jeremy Newkirk, and Kim stood up and yelled for the fun of it. Laura ducked behind her sunglasses.

Every eye in the stands shifted from the high jump pit

to the runners battling for the mile race. Jeremy Newkirk was out in front and close behind him was Clearwater's Aaron Oakman.

As they rounded the final corner, Nicki noticed that Aaron Oakman seemed to shift into high gear. His legs, which had been steadily pumping, moved faster and his arms pushed like pistons.

When Jeremy Newkirk sensed Aaron Oakman sneaking up on his right, he kicked into high gear, too, like a crazy wind-up toy wound too tightly.

"They're sprinting now," Meredith explained to the other girls. "They pace themselves evenly until the end, then they kick in with all they've got and race to the finish line."

Jeremy and Aaron, matched stride for stride, drove themselves toward the finish line. First Aaron edged ahead, then Jeremy. Then Aaron, and in a triumphant burst of speed, Jeremy Newkirk threw back his arms and seemed to push his chest into the tape stretched over the finish line. The Pine Grove Panthers won the race, and the fans in the stands went crazy.

Everyone stomped and cheered but Laura. "I don't why you all are so excited," she said, sighing in exasperation. "What's so great about seeing sweaty guys run around in a circle?"

Nicki looked down at her friend. "You weren't even watching, were you?"

"No," Laura shook her head. "I was too busy watching that skinny girl down there on the field."

As the girls settled back into their seats, Nicki, Christine, Meredith and Kim looked at the girl Laura pointed toward. She was tall and thin, with long dark braids, and she was jumping with excitement. She screamed, "I love you, Jeremy! I love you!" Her shrill voice carried above the noise of the crowd.

"Who is that?" Christine asked, crinkling her nose.

"That is Elinore Anderson," Kim said. "She is in one of my classes. She is in sixth grade."

"She's weird," Christine bluntly remarked. "Why is she carrying on like that?"

"Apparently she loves Jeremy," Laura remarked dryly. "Who wouldn't?"

"Jeremy told me about her," Meredith said, ignoring Laura's comment. "She lives down the street from him and he stopped to help her a few times—you know, he carried her books once. They're both on the track team, so she sees him a lot. Anyway, she lives alone with her mother and she doesn't get much attention, so apparently she has a crush on Jeremy."

"Does he like her?" Nicki asked.

"No, not like that," Meredith explained. "He just feels sorry for her. I told you, he's a nice guy, so he doesn't want to hurt this girl's feelings by telling her to bug off."

Nicki watched as Elinore continued to hop up and down squealing, "I love you, Jeremy. I love you!" Finally Elinore turned and ran over to the girls' coach, looking perfectly happy and content.

"I think they make a perfect couple," Laura said sarcastically. "They're both so skinny they'd have to run around in the shower to get wet."

Christine giggled. "She's so thin, if she had a run in her nylons she'd fall out."

Laura laughed. "She could stand sideways, stick out her tongue and look like a zipper!"

"Cut out the skinny jokes," Meredith said, a little annoyed. "Or I'll start telling jokes about redheads and dumb blondes."

"Oh yeah?" Laura said, tossing her blonde hair. "Give me just one."

"I could give you half a dozen," Meredith answered, raising an eyebrow. "What do you call a blonde who dyes her hair brown?"

Laura and Christine looked at each other and shrugged.

Meredith grinned wickedly. "Artificial intelligence."

"That's not very funny," Laura said, pouting.

"Please do not make fun of each other," Kim said, looking up at Meredith and Laura with her dark eyes. "Let's keep being good friends."

"It's okay," Christine said. "They're not really mad at each other. But I see someone who is — look down there at the Clearwater coach. He's really letting Aaron have it for losing that race!"

The Clearwater coach was standing in front of Aaron Oakman. Aaron sat dejectedly, his head hanging low, and the coach paced up and down in front of him. Nicki couldn't hear what he was saying, but it was obvious he was saying a lot — and loudly, too.

"I'm glad I'm not on that guy's team," Meredith said. "He's really hard on his athletes. And he seems especially hard on his stepson."

Nicki said nothing. She was trying to concentrate on the high jump pit, where Scott and one other jumper were left in competition. Scott ran, jumped — and missed. He and the bar fell into the pit.

Scott wasn't the only one with troubles. In the 100-yard dash, D. N. Downin won for the Pine Grove Panthers, but two steps over the finish line he pitched forward and fell on the asphalt.

"Ouch," Kim said, pointing down at D. N. "He looks hurt."

The coach helped D. N. to his feet, and the girls could see that both knees, his hands, elbows and even his mouth were bloody.

"Ugh," Laura moaned, turning her head away. "I can't stand the sight of blood."

"That's too bad," Meredith said, nodding at the large

scoreboard. "We needed D. N. for the relay. The score is too close. We have to win the relay if we're going to win the track meet."

"What is the relay?" Kim asked.

"The 440 relay," Meredith said. "It's worth seven points and we need it to win the meet. Our four fastest runners will go against Clearwater's four fastest. They run 110 yards each, then hand off the baton to the next runner. The coach will put our fastest runner on the last leg to make up for any time that is lost by the first three runners."

"That means D. N. Downin should have run last, right?" Christine asked.

Meredith nodded. "Yes. But he can't run now. The coach might substitute Jeremy Newkirk, but I don't know. Mile runners don't usually run the relay. That's a lot to ask of anyone."

The meet score was 56-50, with the Clearwater Bulldogs leading. The stands were jammed now with kids and parents who had come from work. Nicki realized that track meets were more popular than she had imagined. Small kids were running up and down the bleachers and others were crawling underneath. One kid a few rows over was dropping chunks of ice through the bleachers onto the little kids below. In the front row, a well-dressed woman was carrying a fussy poodle with bows in his hair and shiny red toenails. People were everywhere, and most of them were concentrating on the last event, the 440 relay.

The two runners for the first leg of the relay were on the field. At the crack of the starter's gun, they were off, and Nicki could see the flash of the silver baton as it caught the sun's rays. The runners concentrated on the track in front of them and seemed to ignore each other and the roar from the crowd.

"POP-corn," a PTA parent yelled in the stands. "Get your POP-corn here."

The second runners got into position, planted their feet firmly and stretched out their arms for the hand-off. Nicki closed her eyes in the risky moment when the baton left the first runner's hand and went into the second. Fortunately, Coach Linton had trained his runners well. They did not drop the baton.

Scott Spence was Pine Grove's third runner. He received his baton smoothly, too, and he and the Clearwater runner seemed to be evenly spaced on the track.

"Go, Scott!" Nicki and Christine cheered together.

"It's going to come down to a race between the Clearwater sprinter and Jeremy," Meredith yelled above the noise of the crowd. "I can't believe Coach Linton is going to use him. He must be exhausted after running the mile."

Jeremy Newkirk got into position in his lane at the bottom of the track, and stretched his hand behind him for the baton. Scott was ten steps away . . . then eight, then five, four, three, two, one—

The entire crowd in the Pine Grove bleachers drew a huge breath and waited for the hand-off, when a shrill, bleating voice broke through the stillness: "Jeremy, I love you!"

Whether he heard it or not, something happened to Jeremy Newkirk. The baton seemed to slide right out of his hand and as he fumbled for it on the hot asphalt of the track, the final Clearwater sprinter flew by, his baton firmly in his grasp.

Jeremy seemed to take forever as he struggled to grab the spinning baton, but finally he had it and began to run. Nicki had never seen legs pump so furiously or a face so determined. His eyes stared straight ahead, his jaws were clenched, and his brown hair flapped like a pair of wings above his head. She could see him breathing hard, and she could almost hear the whoosh, whoosh of his breaths as he kicked and sprinted with every ounce of energy he could muster.

The entire track meet depended on Jeremy Newkirk. All the high jumpers, runners, hurdlers, discus throwers and long jumpers waited to see how he would do. And Jeremy was giving all he had.

At the turn of the track, Jeremy had nearly caught up to the runner from the other team, but he didn't let up. His legs kept pumping and Nicki suddenly realized he could actually win. The finish line was only fifty feet away, and Jeremy Newkirk was coming on strong.

But in the stands, the pampered poodle sprang from his mistress's lap, squirmed through the fence and dashed toward the two boys running around the track. Jeremy Newkirk was racing in the outside lane, and the little dog apparently thought there wouldn't be any harm in chasing a boy who was already running. He cut across the track and flew toward Jeremy, yapping in staccato bursts of noise.

No one was prepared for what happened next. Jeremy saw the dog and screamed in sheer terror. He stopped for a moment, waved his hands helplessly, then turned and ran in the opposite direction, toward the parking lot. Cheered by the attention and noise of the audience, the little dog continued to snip and snap at Jeremy's heels until both dog and boy were off the field.

The sprinter from Clearwater finished his race and curled up on the track, doubled over with laughter. His teammates lifted him to his feet, and the Pine Grove Panthers sat in gloomy silence while the Clearwater Bulldogs celebrated with high fives. The score became official: Clearwater won the race and the meet, 63-50.

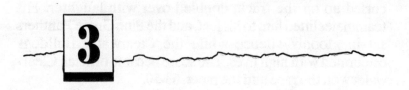

The halls were buzzing with the story at school the next morning.

"Did you see the way Jeremy Newkirk took off with that tiny little dog on his tail?" Corrin Burns asked her friends in homeroom. "What a dweeb he is."

"Yip, yip," Michelle Vander Hagen joked. "I'm a big, ferocious dog. Yip, yip."

"It wasn't funny at all," Jeff Jordan complained. "Thanks to Jeremy Nuthouse, we lost the meet. A lot of people worked hard, only to have that chicken-liver just run off the track because of a dog no bigger than a loaf of bread!"

Nicki had heard enough. "Be quiet, all of you," she snapped at her classmates. "How do you know he wasn't just distracted? He was concentrating really hard, trying his best to win, and then that little dog came along and startled him."

"Don't forget, that wasn't even Jeremy's race. He was filling in for D. N. Downin," Meredith added. "And he had just finished running a mile. Could any of you do better?"

Meredith's remark shut the group up, but Nicki couldn't help feeling glad that she wasn't Jeremy Newkirk. If he dared to come to school at all, it was going to be a rough day.

She did see Jeremy later, walking through the hall with his head down. At his side was Elinore Anderson, as bubbly as a shaken can of pop, but Jeremy wouldn't even look at her as she chatted beside him.

"Look at that!" Christine whispered to Nicki as they passed Jeremy and Elinore. "Elinore's devoted to him, you've got to admit that. The entire school's mad at Jeremy except his one true love!"

"The entire school is *not* mad at him," Nicki corrected her. "We're just disappointed, that's all. I wonder why that little dog spooked him so much?"

Christine shrugged. "It was a frightful little thing. All those bows and ribbons and red nails! But it certainly wasn't anything to make anyone scream in terror and run away!"

"Maybe not you or me," Nicki answered thoughtfully. "But maybe Jeremy has something against poodles."

Christine giggled. "What could anyone have against a *poodle*? For heaven's sake, it was probably named Fifi or Tutu or Doodles. Sounds like a real man-eater to me!"

Nicki just shook her head. "Well, here's my class," Christine said, when they reached the door of the typing lab. "See you later, gator. Unless Pepe the man-eating poodle is on the loose!"

Several kids near the door heard Christine and broke into laughter. Nicki headed down the hall toward her next class. Maybe Jeremy wouldn't mind being the joke of the school. At the next track meet he'd do a good job and that would be the end of it.

The girls met after school at Nicki's locker.

"I love Fridays," Christine said, leaning back against the row of lockers and closing her eyes. "An entire weekend ahead of us with nothing to do."

"I hate weekends," Meredith grumbled, shifting her heavy load of books. "For the exact same reason. I *like* having something to do."

"Well, what are we going to do now?" Laura asked. "Mr. Peterson said he'd take us shopping if we wanted to go. I hear The Gap is having a sale."

Meredith rolled her eyes. "Honestly, Laura, nobody but you ever has any money. And why don't you give Mr. Peterson the afternoon off? We don't need your chauffeur to drive us everywhere. Walking is good for us."

Nicki had to admit that riding in Laura's chauffeur-driven Rolls Royce would be wonderful, especially since the sun was hot outside. "Christine lives closest," she suggested. "Why don't we walk there and just hang out for a while?"

"No," Christine frowned. "You don't want to do that. My aunt and uncle are visiting with their three little kids."

Nicki understood. There were six kids in the Kelshaw family even without visiting relatives, and the house was always crowded. The girls were usually welcome, but Nicki knew that today Mrs. Kelshaw probably wouldn't appreciate four more people coming to visit.

"We could go to my house," Meredith suggested. "It's quiet there, and it's only a little further than Christine's."

"Okay," Nicki agreed.

"Are ya'll sure?" Laura hesitated. "I think it's about ninety degrees out there already. I could call Mr. Peterson, you know. He wouldn't mind coming out to drive us."

"Come on, Laura, stop griping," Christine said,

gathering her books from the floor where she'd dropped them. "Maybe Meredith's mom will let us spend the night."

Laura groaned, but she picked up her bookbag and followed her friends. "You don't know what the sun will do to your complexion," she complained, digging in her purse for her sunglasses as she lagged behind the others. "You'll all have wrinkles before you're thirty."

Nicki and Kim grinned at each other. Laura was spoiled and complained a lot, but she always came through in a pinch. She had been an important part of their mystery-solving team ever since the girls befriended her at the beginning of school.

"Do you think your mom will make Cajun food for us?" Kim asked Meredith as they walked out of the school. "She is a wonderful cook."

"Maybe, if she's not too tired," Meredith answered. "We could always bribe her by cleaning up the house or something."

"Sounds like a fair exchange," Nicki said. "Maybe she'll make jambalaya again."

"With calories galore," Laura grumbled, still trudging along behind the others. "Millions and millions of calories."

"If you hurry up," Meredith called over her shoulder, "you'll burn off those calories and you can eat like a horse tonight."

The girls laughed, except Laura, but she walked faster. "If I keep this up," she said, passing Meredith and Christine, "I'll go out for the track team myself."

That night, after their afternoon of scrubbing the

bathrooms and dusting earned them a wonderful meal of Cajun black beans and rice, the girls relaxed in the living room. Meredith's mother was grading math tests in her den, safely away so the girls wouldn't bother her.

Nicki looked around at her friends and smiled. Each was doing what she enjoyed the most: Kim and Christine were playing Monopoly on the floor, Meredith was in an easy chair reading an encyclopedia, and Laura was studying newspaper ads to find the best Saturday sales.

"Hey, look here," Laura called, folding the newspaper and pointing to a column. "In my horoscope it says that tomorrow I'll begin a new chapter in my life. What do you think that means?"

Meredith frowned. "I can't believe you're reading that stuff. Horoscopes are a waste of time."

Laura slipped off the couch and sat on the floor next to Meredith's chair. "I can't believe you don't read your horoscope, Miss Scientific," she said, pointing to the astrologer's column. "All this stuff is based on science, isn't it?"

"I think you're confusing astrology and astronomy," Meredith said, shifting the heavy encyclopedia on her lap. "They're two different things."

Christine moved her Monopoly shoe to Boardwalk Avenue. "Kim, you'll owe me big bucks if you land here because I'm buying Boardwalk."

"I will not land there," Kim answered, smiling shyly. "But you had better watch out because I am buying all the utilities."

"Forget that dumb game," Laura interrupted. "Listen to me. Nicki, what's your sign?"

Nicki shrugged. "I don't care what my sign is."

Laura insisted. "When is your birthday?"

Christine interrupted. "Listen, Laura, maybe we don't want to mess around with that stuff. My dad told me once that the Bible says it's wrong to put your faith in horoscopes."

"Why is it wrong?" Laura was hurt. "I don't see anything wrong with it. I'm not hurting anyone, for heaven's sake." She leaned back against the easy chair, frowning. "Anyway, there's nothing wrong with what it said. It just said I'm starting a new chapter in my life tomorrow, that's all. What could be wrong with that?"

"Nothing's wrong with that," Nicki tried to explain. "But if tomorrow you go around looking and waiting for it to happen, you've put your faith in the dumb horoscope, that's all."

"I think it's just simple fun," Laura said, twirling a strand of her hair. "It's all perfectly innocent. People like to hear about themselves and what's going to — well, what *could* happen in the future."

The girls were interrupted by a ring from the doorbell. "Who could that be?" Christine asked. "I hope it isn't one of my brothers or sisters. I was looking forward to being away for the night."

Meredith's mother called from the den. "Meredith, honey, would you get that? I'm not expecting anybody."

Meredith went to answer the door and the girls listened quietly. Nicki peeked around the corner and was surprised when Meredith greeted her visitor.

It was Jeremy Newkirk.

4

W hy Jeremy, I didn't expect to see you," Meredith said, opening the door wide. "Do you want to come in? My friends are here, too."

"No, I don't want to come in," Jeremy said, nervously looking past Meredith. "I just wanted to talk to you in private."

"Ooooo," Christine murmured quietly to the other girls. "I think Meredith has an admirer."

"Better not let Elinore Anderson know about it," Laura joked. "She'll come over and squeal Meredith to death."

"Sure, Jeremy, we can talk outside." Meredith shut the door behind her and left the girls in the quiet of the living room.

"What are they saying?" Christine asked, bounding to the window.

"Shhhh," Laura said, putting her ear to the nearest wall. "Maybe we can hear something."

"You can't hear anything that way," Nicki pointed out, moving toward the window. "But at least we can watch."

The girls positioned themselves behind the sheer curtain of the window and looked out. Jeremy and Meredith were sitting on the front step of the porch, and Jeremy nervously handed Meredith an envelope.

"What's that?" Christine asked. "A love note?"

"More likely it's something to do with their science project," Laura said. "He doesn't look like the type to send love notes."

"Why would he want to discuss their science project in private?" Nicki wondered aloud. "We're not in their science class, and we probably wouldn't know what they were talking about, anyway."

"I do not think it has to do with science," Kim remarked, watching quietly. "Look at him — Jeremy looks scared."

Nicki had to admit he did. As Meredith scanned the paper in the envelope, Jeremy Newkirk sat on his hands and nervously bounced his long legs together. He kept looking toward the street, as if he expected someone or something to appear at any moment.

Meredith folded the paper and placed it back in the envelope. She said something to Jeremy, but he shook his head and took the envelope away from her. Meredith kept talking, and once she gestured toward the house. Finally, Jeremy handed the envelope to her and stood up.

Meredith smiled at him and Jeremy tried to smile back. Nicki thought he seemed only a little relieved, though, because he kept his hands in his pockets and kept nervously jiggling from head to toe.

When Meredith said goodbye and came back in the house, the girls bombarded her with questions.

"New boyfriend, Meredith?"

"What's the letter?"

"What did he want?"

"Why is he so nervous?"

Meredith plopped down on the couch and held the envelope in her lap. "No, he's not my boyfriend, he's my lab partner. He's scared because of this letter. He heard about our last mystery and thought maybe we could help him."

Nicki smiled. The girls' last mystery, *The Case of the Teenage Terminator*, had solved a big problem at Pine Grove High School. Jeremy must have heard about it from one of the guys.

"Why wouldn't he come in?" Christine asked. "Doesn't he trust us?"

"I don't know," Meredith shrugged. "Jeremy wants help, but he doesn't want anyone else to know about this. I managed to convince him we could help him."

"Another mystery?" Nicki was dying of curiosity. "What's in the letter?"

"I'll show you." Meredith pointed to the envelope. "First, notice that this came in the ordinary U. S. mail. It's addressed to Jeremy Newkirk, with his address. The typewriting is typical. Any one of a million typewriters could have done this."

"There's no return address," Nicki pointed out. "What about the postmark?"

"It's postmarked 'Pine Grove, Florida,' so the envelope could have been mailed by anyone in Pine Grove," Meredith said. "It was mailed yesterday, and Jeremy received it this morning."

"Fingerprints?" Laura asked.

"None that are visible," Meredith answered. "I guess there are lots of invisible ones, but we're not exactly set up to fingerprint everyone in town."

Laura rolled her eyes. "Of course not. But if we have to give it to the police, they could do it."

Meredith shrugged. "Indubitably. But I don't think this is a matter for the police — yet."

"Okay, let's get on with it," Christine snapped. "What's in the envelope?"

Meredith carefully withdrew a sheet of paper from the envelope. "Notice this is regular notebook paper," she said, unfolding the sheet. "The kind everybody uses."

"Noted," Kim answered.

Meredith smoothed the sheet of paper and laid it on the coffee table. The girls gasped at what they saw.

On a regular sheet of notebook paper, someone had taped a picture of a snarling dog. His fangs were bared, saliva was drooling from his mouth and his eyes were slits of fury.

At the bottom of the page, someone had typed:

`For you on March 22.`

"What does that mean?" Christine asked, her eyes wide. "Someone's getting him a dog?"

"Maybe someone's just trying to tease him about yesterday," Laura said. "Absolutely everyone has heard about him running away from that dinky poodle."

"I don't think this is meant to tease him," Nicki said thoughtfully. "That dog looks threatening, not funny."

"What is March 22?" Kim asked.

Meredith shook her head. "I don't know. It's next Saturday, but Jeremy didn't say anything about it."

"Does he have any idea who might have sent this?" Nicki asked.

Meredith shook her head. "No. But he's scared to death. He's a cynophobe."

"A sign-oh-what?" Christine crinkled her nose. "Is it contagious?"

Meredith shook her head. "He has cynophobia. An unreasonable, irrational fear of dogs." She tapped the fierce-looking picture with her fingernail. "Someone really knew how to push Jeremy's button and upset him. Jeremy hates dogs."

Christine threw her head up indignantly. "He hates dogs? How could anyone in the world hate dogs? They're the most wonderful, loving animals on the face of the earth!"

"Maybe for you they are," Nicki said, "but some people just aren't wild about them. Not everyone has a zoo in their house like you do, either."

"Well, Jeremy doesn't exactly hate them," Meredith went on, "he's just scared of them. Really scared."

"That's crazy," Christine shook her head. "I don't understand it."

"You aren't supposed to understand it," Meredith said. "It's his phobia, not yours."

"Well, not only do we have to find out who sent this note and why," Nicki said, gently fingering the page, "but it wouldn't hurt if we helped Jeremy get over his fear of dogs, would it?"

Laura laughed. "You'd better start him with something small, like a Chihuahua," she said. She pointed to the picture of the snarling dog. "After seeing what a tiny poodle did to Jeremy, imagine what would happen if he met this killer on the street!"

5

The first thing we have to do," Nicki said, settling down on the carpet and crossing her legs, "is interview Jeremy. There are still too many things we don't know. Is someone mad at him? Who knows that he doesn't like dogs?"

"The whole world knows," Laura said dryly. "If they didn't see him running at that track meet they heard about it at school."

"Okay, so lots of people know," Nicki said. "But remember: Whoever sent this note was either teasing or serious. And whoever our mystery person is, he or she must have two things—"

"Motive and opportunity," Kim recited. "Every good detective knows that."

Nicki nodded. "That's right. So Meredith, do you think Jeremy will come back over and talk to us?"

Meredith looked doubtful. "I don't know. He's really shy. I almost couldn't get him to leave the note so I could show it to you guys. He's embarrassed, too, about the track meet."

"Tell him we're not going to make fun of him. We want to help," Nicki said. "Call him now, before it gets too late. Ask him if he can come over right away."

Meredith got up to go make the phone call in the kitchen, and Christine followed her. "Does your mom have any leftover red beans and rice in the fridge?" Christine asked. "Isn't it about time for a snack?"

"That sounds good to me," Laura said, laughing, and she and Kim darted into the kitchen, too. Nicki sat quietly, looking carefully at the note Jeremy Newkirk had received. No return address. Plain white envelope, the kind you buy in a drugstore. Ordinary notebook paper, with ordinary scotch tape holding the picture of the snarling dog.

But the picture—where had it come from? Nicki carefully tried to pry the picture off the notebook paper by lifting a taped edge. The notebook paper tore, but Nicki was able to peel the paper off the back of the picture.

"Destroying evidence?" Meredith asked, sneaking up behind Nicki's shoulder.

Nicki jumped, then held the paper up for Meredith to see. "I thought maybe it would help if we found out where the picture was from," Nicki said.

"Hmmmm." Meredith took the paper and peeled the picture away further. "There's a magazine article on the back, and it seems to be an article about the Supreme Court. I'm not positive, but it looks like the type used in *Newsweek* magazine."

"Are you sure?" Nicki asked.

Meredith nodded. "My dad subscribes to *Newsweek*. If we went to the library, I bet I could find the exact issue this article is in. The dog picture must be part of an article or something on the other side."

Christine heard what they were saying as she came into the room. "That dog is part of an article?" She made a face. "Why in the world would he be in *Newsweek*?"

Nicki shrugged. "We won't know for sure until we find the magazine."

"We can go to the library tomorrow," Meredith said, "after we've talked to Jeremy."

"He's not coming tonight?" Laura asked, settling back onto the couch with a bowl of warmed-over red beans and rice.

"No, he doesn't want to come out after dark," Meredith said simply. "He's coming over first thing in the morning."

"Is he afraid of the dark, too?" Kim asked, her eyes wide.

"No," Meredith said. "But there might be a dog hiding in the dark."

Nicki could hardly open her eyes the next morning, even when Meredith's mom stood in the doorway and shouted that it was ten o'clock and time for all girls to be up and out of bed. They had stayed awake until two, watching old movies on television, and they had laughed so much Nicki's voice was hoarse.

"It is time to hurry up," Kim called, sticking her head into the room. Nicki was surprised that Kim was already dressed. Since when was she an early riser?

"What's your hurry?" mumbled Christine, glaring up at Kim through strands of red hair.

"Jeremy Newkirk is here," Kim replied, smiling. "In the living room."

"Ohmigoodness," Christine yelped, diving back into

her sleeping bag. Her muffled voice came out of the bag: "I can't let any boy see me like this."

Meredith smiled and waved at Kim. "Go keep him company, Kimmie, until we're dressed," she said. "Feed him a doughnut or anything you can find. There's a pizza in the fridge, I think."

"No, there's not," Laura answered, sleepily sitting up. "We finished that off last night, too."

"Just keep him busy," Nicki said. "We'll be out in a minute."

By the time Meredith, Christine, Nicki and Laura had dressed and brushed their hair, Kim and Jeremy had become good friends. *At least he'll talk to Kim*, Nicki thought. *That's good. He's got to feel he can trust us.*

"And I'd like more than anything to write scripts for the Star Trek series," Jeremy was telling Kim as the girls walked in. "I love science fiction. Have you ever read any of — " Jeremy saw the girls and abruptly stopped talking.

"Jeremy, you know everybody, don't you?" Meredith asked. "Nicki Holland, Christine Kelshaw and Laura Cushman?"

"I've seen them around," Jeremy mumbled, still looking down.

"Well, we'd like to help you get to the bottom of this mystery," Nicki said gently, sitting next to Jeremy on the couch. "But we need to know a few things first."

"Like what?" Jeremy looked up and squinted behind his glasses.

"Well, like, does anyone hate you?" Christine asked bluntly from the easy chair.

Jeremy blushed and looked down at the carpet again.

"I'm not the most popular guy in school, if that's what you mean," he said. "But I can't think of anyone who *hates* me."

"I don't know why anyone would," Meredith said, smiling. She sat on the floor and reached over to pat his well-worn sneakers. "You're a nice guy, Jeremy."

Jeremy shook his head.

"Okay, what about this date?" Nicki pulled out the menacing letter and Jeremy shuddered when he glanced over at the snarling dog. "What happens on March 22?" Nicki asked. "Anything special?"

"Nothing special to most people," Jeremy said, shrugging. "But I'm running a five-mile race on that day."

"Ugh," Laura muttered.

Meredith ignored her. "Tell us about the race, Jeremy."

"It's a distance run for the three middle schools in the county," Jeremy said. "Anyone on the track team can go out for it. The prize is a trophy for the school and $200 for the winner."

The snarling dog picture was beginning to make more sense to Nicki. Someone knew Jeremy Newkirk was afraid of dogs, and someone knew that his race would be terribly upset if he thought a dog would be anywhere near. But why would anyone go through all this trouble for a skinny kid like Jeremy Newkirk?

"This may sound really dumb," Nicki said, nodding at Jeremy, "but I don't know much about track." She paused. "Are you any good?"

Meredith laughed. "I think what Nicki means, Jeremy, is why would anyone go through all this trouble to scare you away from the race? Are you a threat for any specific runner?"

Jeremy shrugged and his face turned a little red. "I dunno," he mumbled. "All I know is I've got the best mile time in the county. No one has beat me yet in the mile race."

Nicki and Meredith looked at each other. Jeremy was really good, then, and he was a threat to *everybody* running in the race.

"Can you think of anyone who would want to scare you out of the race?" Nicki asked gently. "A certain competitor, perhaps? Someone on the Pine Grove team?"

Jeremy shook his head. "None of the guys on my team would want to scare me. At least," he blushed again, "I don't *think* they're still mad at me about the other day."

"Well, it's a useless threat, anyway," Christine said. "Someone may have meant to scare you with this note, but what are they going to do? Run along beside you with some kind of mangy mutt? There's no way a dog can hurt you, so you can just ignore the letter and go on with your race."

Meredith snapped her fingers. "Unless—" she turned to Jeremy. "Where is this race, Jeremy?"

"It's a race through town," he said. "It starts in Clearwater and ends somewhere in Pine Grove."

"Where through town?"

Jeremy shrugged. "We won't get a map until the Monday before the race. The track coaches of the three schools will lay out the route, and then we'll have a week to practice running it if we want to." He laughed. "I'll run anywhere except on Logan Lane. You know, there's a dog there that looks sort of like this one in the picture."

"Don't worry, we'll go through the course with you," Nicki promised. "Just to make sure the race course isn't through the dog pound or something."

"Well, I'm not running it," Laura stated flatly. She stood up and stretched. "There's no way you're going to get me outside and in a sweat."

"You can ride in your limo," Christine said. She winked at Jeremy. "Maybe Elinore Anderson will run it with us."

At the mention of Elinore's name, Jeremy's eyebrows rushed together and he frowned. "Forget it," he said, a note of anger in his voice. "Forget this whole thing. Is this her idea? Did she call you and tell you to bring me here? Have you got her hidden somewhere, maybe back in the bedroom? Honestly, that girl is driving me crazy."

"What are you talking about?" Meredith asked, raising an eyebrow. "We haven't talked to Elinore at all. We just saw her the other day, and it was obvious that she really likes you. Christine was just teasing, Jeremy."

Jeremy shook his head and sighed. "Sorry. I guess I'm paranoid. But Thursday night after that horrible meet I finally told her to leave me alone. But she still hangs around."

Laura snapped her fingers. "Need we hear more?" she asked. "A jealous female sends a vicious letter in the mail to the guy who spurned her love. It's that simple."

Nicki crinkled her forehead in thought. Was it? Could Elinore Anderson have played such a trick?

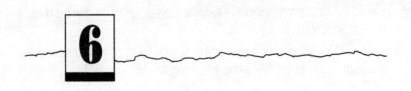

6

"Is there anyone besides Elinore Anderson who would want to scare Jeremy?" Nicki asked after Jeremy had left.

"I know," Christine said. "Maybe he's wrong about the other kids on his team. Maybe someone is really steamed about his losing the track meet for us the other day, and this little note is just one way of getting even."

"That's possible," Nicki said. "But if I understand it right, this five-mile race isn't like a meet where everyone depends on everyone else for points. It's more like 'winner take all.' It seems like anyone on the track team would be thrilled if Jeremy won the trophy for our school."

"Unless they want the $200 for themselves," Laura pointed out.

"We know that whoever sent this note has access to a *Newsweek* magazine," Meredith said, holding up the mysterious letter.

"That could be anybody," Kim said softly. "That magazine is in the library. The mystery person could have ripped the page out."

"Know who I suspect?" Christine said, her green eyes gleaming. "D. N. Downin. Jeremy was running in his place when he turned tail and lost the track meet."

"Maybe D. N. plans to run in the five-mile race and

wants Jeremy out of the way," Laura added. "He wants to get rid of his competition."

"Will D. N. be healed up by then?" Kim asked. "He was hurt badly in the track meet."

"Skinned knees and a bloody nose, that's about all," Meredith replied. "I saw him at school yesterday and he was fine. He acted like he deserved a Purple Heart or something for his injuries. And D. N.'s a sprinter, not a distance runner. There's no way he could win unless Jeremy doesn't run."

Nicki reached into her purse for her little black notebook. "What do we know about the culprit?" she asked, writing as she talked. "We know these things:

1. The culprit knows Jeremy is afraid of dogs.

2. The culprit knows about the race on March 22.

3. The culprit has access to a *Newsweek* and a typewriter.

4. The culprit has hostile intentions."

"Hostile intentions?" Laura said, her eyes growing wide. "That sounds so serious. How do we know this isn't all a joke?"

"A joke is when you say 'boo' to startle someone else," Nicki said, putting down her pencil. She looked at the notebook. "Do we know anything else?"

"The culprit must have motive and opportunity," Kim said.

"That's right," Nicki said, turning to a clean page. "So who are our best suspects?"

Laura spoke up first. "I vote for Elinore Anderson, jealous girlfriend."

"I vote for D. N. Downin," Christine said. "But I don't

think he means to hurt Jeremy. I think he's just trying to scare off his competition."

"That's a good motive," Nicki said, writing the suspects in her notebook. "Anyone else?"

"Anyone on the track team," Kim said, "if they are upset about losing the track meet."

"Corrin Burns and Jeff Jordan were plenty steamed in homeroom the other day," Meredith said. "And remember how Corrin sent Kim those notes when we were solving the case of the mystery mark? This sounds like something she would do."

Nicki added those names then snapped her notebook shut.

"Where do we go from here?" Christine asked.

"I think we go to the library," Nicki said. "We ought to find out some things about track, and running, and cynophobia. Then we ought to find the *Newsweek* with the picture of our precious pup in it." She looked up at the other girls. "Can we meet there this afternoon?"

Everyone nodded. Laura looked down at the letter and shivered. "I really don't blame Jeremy for being upset about this," she said. She nodded at the picture of the raging dog. "If I ran into this man-eater, I'd be scared, too."

All the girls were at the local public library by three o'clock—except Laura.

"Where is that girl?" Nicki said, looking out toward the parking lot. "What could be keeping her?"

"Maybe she's having her Saturday manicure," Christine said, laughing. "You never know about Laura."

The silver flash of the Cushman's limo appeared in the street before them. "Finally," Meredith sighed, turning to go indoors. "Here she comes."

Laura bounded out of the limo before Mr. Peterson even had a chance to open the door. "Hey, you guys," she squealed in delight. "Guess who I met in the drugstore?"

"Who?" Christine asked.

"Aaron Oakman. Remember the good-looking runner from Clearwater Middle School? The blonde guy who almost beat Jeremy Newkirk at the track meet?"

"Oh yeah," Nicki said. "I remember. You were drooling over him."

"Almost," Laura grinned. "Anyway, remember my horoscope said a new chapter in my life would begin today? Well, there I was, picking out a new shade of fingernail polish, when I looked up and there he was! So I went over and told him I'd seen him run, and that I'm a good friend of Jeremy Newkirk's, and congratulations on winning the track meet, and then guess what?"

"What?" Nicki was bored already. Honestly, Laura was so boy crazy!

"He said I ought to go running with him sometime. He said we could meet at the park after school and run on one of those fitness trails."

Christine threw back her head and laughed. "I don't believe you, Laura. You hate running! You hate sweating! How in the world do you think you could keep up with Aaron Oakman?"

Laura looked hurt. "It's just running. How hard can it be? Besides," she bit her lip playfully and her eyes sparkled,

"I don't care if we actually run together or not. It's enough just to know that he *wants* me to go running with him."

She tossed her blonde hair and walked into the library. Nicki and Meredith gave each other "here-we-go-again" looks, and the five of them set out to work.

7

An hour later, Kim held up a copy of *Newsweek* and waved at Nicki: "I found it!"

The other girls scurried to her table. Kim pointed to a page in the magazine with an article on the Supreme Court, then turned the page. There was the vicious dog in Jeremy's letter, in full, blazing color.

"It's an ad for Iron Man Cologne," Meredith sniffed, frowning in distaste. "How disgusting!"

" 'When manly just isn't enough,' " Nicki read the advertising slogan. The entire photograph showed a rugged-looking man dressed in hunting camouflage, holding the killer dog on a leash while it growled and snarled at a startled bear.

Laura shrugged. "I like Iron Man," she said. She elbowed Christine. "That's what your brother wears, isn't it?"

"How on earth should I know?" asked Christine, bewildered. "All I know is you can smell him from ten feet away when he's ready to go on a date."

Meredith and Kim burst into giggles, and the librarian looked over at them from her desk.

"Shhhh," Meredith whispered, controlling her laughter. She took a deep breath. "Now, let's look closely here. What issue is this magazine?"

"It's the March 10 issue," Nicki said, looking at the cover. "It's really recent."

"Okay. So whoever sent the letter just saw this picture and cut it out. Since it's a recent issue, it's not like he — "

"Or she," Laura interrupted.

Meredith glared at Laura, but kept talking, " — or she — had to dig for it. Our mystery mailer just saw the picture, thought of Jeremy, and cut it out."

"Maybe the person uses Iron Man cologne and had seen the picture before," Christine offered. "Does anyone know if D. N. Downin wears Iron Man?"

"I don't think we can assume the person uses Iron Man cologne," Nicki pointed out. "It's possible, but he — or she — wouldn't *have* to. Anyone could cut this picture out of a magazine."

The other girls nodded in agreement. "This doesn't really help us much, does it?" Christine asked, looking again at the ad in the magazine.

"It could," Meredith offered. "For one thing, not everybody reads *Newsweek*. And I think we're looking here at someone who has it delivered to their home. I don't think our mystery person would cut up a library's copy, so he or she must have cut it from a magazine at home."

"How about at a doctor's office?" Christine said. "What if D. N. Downin went to the doctor and saw *Newsweek* there?"

"Think a minute, Christine," Nicki said. "If you were at the doctor's office and there were magazines all around, would you pick up *Newsweek*?"

"I would," Meredith volunteered.

Christine giggled. "I wouldn't. I'd read *Seventeen*, then *People*, then maybe *Good Housekeeping*."

"Just because Christine is scatter-brained doesn't mean our mystery person is," Laura whispered. "Maybe she—"

"Or he," Meredith inserted.

"Okay, maybe whoever it is does read *Newsweek*. We don't know. Maybe it's Elinore Anderson and under all that goofiness, she's really smart. Maybe her mom is a teacher or doctor or something and she has to read it."

Nicki rolled her eyes. "I think we've covered this subject. We know that the ad came from *Newsweek*, and that it was an ad for Iron Man cologne. That's all we can know for sure at this point. We'll just have to wait to find out any more."

Back at school on Monday, Nicki was amazed that Laura wasn't floating through the halls. Aaron Oakman had called her on Sunday and they were planning to meet at the park on Monday afternoon to run together. Laura was in love—again—and Nicki and the others found the whole thing a little crazy.

"I mean it's one thing to like a boy and another to go as loony as Laura has," Christine said at lunch. "By next week she'll tell us they're getting married."

"I will not," answered Laura in a lofty tone. "I'm not getting married until after college."

Kim was opening a Tupperware bowl of something from home, and Meredith was fascinated. "What is that stuff?" she asked. "I hate to tell you, Kim, but it doesn't look very appetizing."

Kim blushed. "It is kimchee," she said. "A Korean dish. Everyone in my family eats it." She shrugged gently. "We love it."

"Ugh," Christine said, glancing in the bowl. "I guess it's something you have to learn to like."

"An acquired taste," Kim smiled. "But it is good for you."

"I can't say this pizza looks any better," Meredith said, looking down at the round circle of stiff dough on her tray.

Nicki bit into her tuna sandwich, brought from home. "Forget the food for a minute," she said, taking time to swallow. "Has anyone heard anything about Jeremy?"

Meredith shook her head. "I saw him in science this morning and he was fine. He said nothing had happened since we talked to him last, so maybe it's no big deal. Maybe it was just a one-time thing."

"Maybe." Nicki took another bite of her sandwich. Maybe that letter was just someone's way of getting back at Jeremy for running from that poodle at the track meet. Maybe nothing would come of it.

"Has Elinore Anderson done anything else weird?" Laura asked.

"I am in Elinore's math class," Kim said. "She was there today and did nothing strange. She seemed quiet, but okay. She talked to me a little while."

"Did she say anything about Jeremy?" Laura asked.

Kim smiled shyly. "Yes. She said she liked Jeremy very much and that he was nice and a very good runner."

"Anything else?" Christine wanted to know.

Kim thought. "She said something about wanting to

run a race this weekend, but she wanted to watch Jeremy rather than run it herself."

"Kim," Nicki put her sandwich down. "You know that thing you can do where you remember voices? Can you remember exactly what and how Elinore said that stuff about the race?"

Since they had met her, the girls had been fascinated by Kim's ability to remember exactly what people said and how they said it. Meredith called Kim's gift "total vocal recall."

Kim nodded and closed her eyes. A few seconds later, the girls heard Kim mimic Elinore perfectly. It was like Elinore was there with them. "You know there's a big race next weekend and girls can run, too," Kim recited. "But I'd rather watch Jeremy run. He's so nice, don't you think? He's just the best. I think he likes me, but he's really shy. Have you noticed? I don't know what I'm going to do, but somehow, someday, that boy's gonna know that I just love him to death."

Kim opened her eyes. "That is it," she said in her own voice.

"Talk about boy crazy," Laura raised her eyebrows and shook her finger at the other girls. "I told you," she said. "Elinore Anderson will do anything to get Jeremy to notice her. You just heard what she said."

"I don't know," Meredith said slowly. "She didn't sound angry. She sounded, well, sincere."

"Sincerely goofy, you mean," Christine added. "The girl is imagining all kinds of things."

"Maybe she's not angry now, but she was last week when Jeremy told her to get lost," Laura added.

"Maybe," Nicki said, throwing the crusts of her bread

into her lunch bag. "Kim, you keep an eye on Elinore for us. And Meredith, can't you get Jeremy to talk to us again? I think we should get to know him a little better."

"I don't think he wants anything else to do with us," Meredith said. "I mean, nothing else has happened and he probably thinks it's all over. He told me this morning he just wants to forget all about that horrible letter."

"Maybe we can go where he is," Nicki offered. "What does he do in the afternoons?"

"That's easy," Meredith said, smiling. "The track team is meeting at Pine Grove Park every afternoon this week for practice. Jeremy will be there running the fitness run."

"No," Laura gasped. "There'll be an entire team of people at the park with Aaron and me?" She looked at her friends. "And all of you are going to be there, too, aren't you?"

Meredith grinned. "Laura, we wouldn't miss this for the world."

8

The park was crowded that afternoon. Not only had the entire Pine Grove track team come over on a school bus, but there were mothers with their children in the kiddie playground, adults in sweat headbands running the fitness trails, and lots of kids like Nicki and her friends who just wanted a place to hang out.

The girls found a picnic table and hopped up on it.

"Look at all the initials carved into this table," Christine said, studying the table top. "Here's a N. H. + S. S., Nicki," she teased. "Could that be Nicki Holland and Scott Spence?"

"Not hardly," Nicki said, looking around for Scott. Had he come over, too? "We're just good friends."

Nicki finally spotted Scott—he was with Jeremy Newkirk near the chin-up bars. "Has anyone seen Laura?" she asked casually. "I want to get a closer look at her dream guy."

"Miss Romantic and her latest flame are over there near the swings," Meredith said, jerking her head in the direction of the playground. "I knew he wouldn't be able to get that girl to run on the trail. She's probably stalling for time so she won't have to run."

Nicki laughed. "Maybe she's doing his horoscope. I thought she'd get tired of that stuff, but this morning she said she and Aaron were sure to be compatible because she was a Scorpio and he was a Taurus."

"That's so silly," Christine said, watching Laura and Aaron. "But I have to admit they look good together. A cute couple."

Meredith rolled her eyes. "Brother. Let's not forget why we're here. But honestly, Nicki, I don't think Jeremy is going to come talk to us. He'll just hang around with his teammates until it's time to go."

"That's okay," Nicki answered, leaning forward, her chin in her hands. "Sometimes you can learn a lot just by watching people."

There was a lot to see. D. N. Downin was apparently a devoted athlete—he was running alone down the fitness trail and pushing himself hard. Jeremy Newkirk was more sociable, although he spent a lot of his time with Scott and ducked his head shyly whenever he caught Nicki or any of her friends looking in his direction. Coach Linton was relaxed on a bench under a tree, letting his athletes do what they pleased to train for the big race.

Nicki found her eyes wandering back to Laura and Aaron. Aaron seemed not to care much about the race; he was giving Laura his full attention. They were sitting on swings next to each other, and Laura was talking a mile a minute. Aaron was nodding and smiling, and every once in a while he'd get up and push Laura high so that she laughed and shrieked and begged him to stop.

Nicki couldn't help wondering what it would be like if she and Scott were on the swings. They had always been good friends and able to talk to each other, but Scott was always so busy with one thing or another and she was always working on a mystery . . .

"Uh oh," Christine's voice interrupted her thoughts. "What if Jeremy Newkirk gets a look at this!"

Nicki turned from watching Aaron and Laura and saw a man in the park leading the biggest, most muscular dog she had ever seen.

"What is that?" she whispered, fascinated.

"It's a mastiff," Meredith answered matter-of-factly. "It's the biggest dog God ever made. They can weigh over 200 pounds and have the strength of six men."

"He is so *ugly*," Kim whispered. "Look at that pushed-in face."

"I think he's adorable," Christine answered. "But he's so big! I'll bet he eats as much in one meal as my dog does in a week!"

"Thankfully, they are very gentle dogs," Meredith said, hopping down from the table. "But Jeremy probably won't want to stand around and hear about it. Someone ought to go over there and warn him."

Nicki hopped off the table, too. "I don't want to be around if Jeremy sees that dog coming his way," she said, laughing nervously. "If he ran from a poodle, he'd probably faint if he saw this big guy."

"That man is taking his dog over to the trees," Kim said. "So we can probably stay between him and Jeremy."

The girls walked quickly toward the two boys.

"Hi, Scott," Nicki called, not wanting to embarrass Jeremy. She positioned herself carefully between the dog and the boys, noticing that the other girls were trying to keep Jeremy's attention focussed away from the trees where the man and his dog were walking. "How's it going, you guys?"

Scott grinned. "Fine. I haven't seen you in a while."

Nicki felt herself turning red. "I know. Things have been busy. I mean, you've been at track practice and all . . ."

"Nicki," Meredith interrupted. "Remember why we came over here?"

"Yeah." Nicki bit her lower lip and turned to Jeremy. "Jeremy," she explained calmly, "we don't want you to get upset or anything, but there's a very nice, very gentle dog in the park."

"What?" Jeremy smiled a wooden smile, but Nicki could see fear in his eyes.

"It's a mastiff, and they're quite large," Meredith said, measuring an imaginary dog in the air. "You could even say they're enormous, but he won't bother you."

"This could be good for you," Christine quipped. "If you just could get used to dogs, you would see they are okay. I mean there are a few that aren't so nice, but . . . "

"STOP THAT DOG!" a man's voice boomed behind them.

Nicki turned around just in time to see the man with the mastiff fall flat on his face. The huge dog, his blubbery jowls flapping with each bounding leap, was chasing something through the grass. He was free of his leash and having the time of his life.

Nicki jerked back around to check on Jeremy. He was still standing, his hands on the chin up bar, but he was clenching the bar so tightly his knuckles were white. Beads of perspiration broke out on his upper lip and forehead.

"It's okay, Jeremy," Nicki said. "That dog's just chasing something through the grass. A bird, maybe, or a frog."

But Jeremy wasn't listening. His wide eyes were staring past Nicki at something and when she looked, Nicki saw the dog zigging and zagging through the grass and coming in their direction.

Christine began to squeal in spite of herself. "Nick-iiiiii," she squeaked. "Are you sure he's a nice dog?"

As if in answer, the dog pounced and stopped ten feet in front of them. As they watched in horror, the humongous animal lowered his head in the grass, then triumphantly lifted a rabbit in its jaws.

"Oh no, the poor thing," Christine whispered, then she marched out to the dog. "Put it down, dog! Put that rabbit down!"

The 200-pound dog wasn't about be ordered about by an unfamiliar ninety-pound girl. As if in defiance, he shook the rabbit from side to side, until the rabbit was limp in his mouth.

"Don't look, Nicki," Scott said. "The poor thing was probably dead the minute the dog grabbed it."

"Don't blame the dog," Meredith said. "It was only obeying its natural instincts."

The dog's breathless owner came running up, muttering under his breath. "Drop it," he ordered, and the dog meekly lay the dead rabbit at his master's feet. His ears went back and his tail lowered between his legs.

"You see, Jeremy," Nicki said, turning around. "Even dogs as big as that obey their masters. He wasn't really bad."

But Jeremy was no longer standing by the chin-up bar. He was sitting on the ground, his knees drawn tightly to him, and he was shivering.

"Get . . . it . . . out . . . of . . . here," he whispered through teeth that were clenched tightly. "Mmmm-make it go away."

Jeremy Newkirk looked more like a scared two-year-old than a champion track star.

9

Don't worry, Jeremy, we're going to help you," Meredith said, taking Jeremy by the arm and pulling him to his feet. "You just tough it out and we'll get you through this."

Christine shook her head in disbelief. "That dog wasn't going to hurt you," she said, a note of impatience in her voice. "Honestly, Jeremy."

Scott tried to lighten the mood: "Come on, Jeremy, that's no way to act in front of the girls!"

Jeremy swallowed hard and his eyes caught Kim's for a second. "Sorry," he said, lowering his head again. "I just can't help it."

"There's got to be a way to get you over your cynophobia," Meredith said, tapping her forehead thoughtfully.

"What'd she say?" Scott asked, looking at Nicki.

"Jeremy has a fear of dogs," Nicki explained. "Meredith wants to cure him."

"Oh." Scott looked at his teammate curiously. "Well, I don't think I can help. My dog, Mack, is nearly as big as that mastiff we just saw."

"No, we need to expose him to dogs little by little," Meredith said. "Maybe we should take him to a pet store. There are lots of dogs there, and they're all in cages."

"That's a great idea!" Christine said, clapping her hands. "When can we go?"

"As soon as possible, I think," Nicki said, looking Jeremy over. He was still pale and a little shaky on his feet, but he was okay.

"Should we get Laura to call Mr. Peterson?" Meredith asked. "He said he'd be happy to give us a ride anytime we needed to go anywhere."

"I'll go see if I can tear Laura away from Mr. Wonderful," Christine mumbled, turning to walk toward the playground. "Wish me luck."

Coach Linton took one look at pale Jeremy Newkirk and agreed that an afternoon off might be a good idea. "Get him out of the sun and make sure he gets some rest," the coach told Scott. "What's wrong with him, anyway? The boy looks like he's seen a ghost."

"It's okay, Coach," Scott explained. "A big dog just came out of nowhere and scared him."

"Unbelievable." The coach shook his head and kicked the dirt in frustration. "Jeremy," he said, pausing for the right words, "you've just got to get over this thing. Be a man! It's just not normal for a healthy, red-blooded American boy to be afraid of man's best friend!"

Jeremy's face fell and he didn't look up.

"We'd better go now," Nicki said. "We'll take good care of him, I promise." The three of them walked over to the picnic tables where Meredith and Kim were waiting for Laura.

Kim looked anxiously at Jeremy. "Are you feeling better now?" she asked.

"Yeah, I am," Jeremy said, smiling quickly at Kim.

"Don't look, but here comes Christine with Laura," Meredith whispered to Nicki. "And Aaron Oakman is with her."

"Hey, have you all met Aaron Oakman?" Laura breezed into the group. "Aaron, these are all my friends I've been telling you about—Nicki, Meredith, Kim, Scott and Jeremy."

Nicki, Meredith and Kim smiled at Aaron, but Scott and Jeremy just stared at him.

Aaron cleared his throat uncomfortably. "Hey, that was some race the other day," he said, nodding at Jeremy. "I tried my best to beat you, but I just couldn't do it."

"Well, you won the track meet," Scott said easily, sensing that Jeremy didn't want to talk about the awful meet with Clearwater. "But we'll catch you next time."

"Say Aaron, are you running in the five-mile race that's coming up?" Meredith asked, smiling pleasantly.

"Uh, maybe," Aaron said, turning to wink at Laura. "If there's nothing else to do."

Laura blushed. "Well, you'd better get to running," she said sweetly. "Isn't that why you came out here to the park today?"

"It's only part of the reason," he said, bending down to her ear. He whispered loudly: "I'll call you later tonight."

"Okay," Laura answered. She sighed as Aaron walked away, and Nicki saw Meredith turn her head and make a gagging motion. Honestly, Laura's love life was enough to make anyone nauseous!

When Aaron was safely away, Laura turned on her friends: "Don't you think you were all a little rude to him?"

"We tried to be nice, but he's the enemy, remember?" Christine said. "What'd you want us to do, jump up and give him a kiss? You can't expect us to get all excited over somebody from *Clearwater!*"

"This 'enemy' stuff is for children," Laura answered, flipping her hair over her shoulder. "If you were really mature, you wouldn't care where a person is from. Things like that just don't matter to me."

"They matter to me when the guy is my top competition in the race," Jeremy said, jumping down from the top of the picnic table. "I've never trusted Aaron Oakman."

"That's simply ridiculous. You don't even know him," Laura snapped. "You're just jealous because he and his team won the track meet last week while you ran away from a ten-pound puppy."

As soon as the words were out of her mouth, Laura's eyes widened in horror. "Oh, I'm sorry," she said, clapping her hand over her mouth. "I didn't mean it, Jeremy, I really didn't."

Meredith gave Laura a how-could-you-be-so-dumb look. "Laura's letting her mouth run away with her," she said, looking over at Jeremy. "But we really want to help you. Come with us this afternoon to the pet store and we'll help you get used to dogs. You've just never been around them, that's all."

Nicki looked at Laura. "Do you really want to help?"

Laura, her hands still across her mouth, nodded dumbly.

"Then will you call Mr. Peterson and ask if he'll take us to the pet store?"

Laura nodded again and lowered her hands from her mouth. "Sure. And Jeremy, I'm really sorry. Honestly. My horoscope today told me to watch my mouth. I should have. I promise I won't say another word about you-know-what. And nobody thinks you're a coward. They just don't know that you—"

"Laura," Meredith interrupted. "Go to the phone. Now."

"Okay," Laura answered meekly. She and Kim hurried to the pay phone while the others waited for Mr. Peterson and the silver Rolls Royce.

Nicki loved pet shops. From the moment she opened the door and sniffed the peculiar mingled smells of cedar shavings, birds and furry creatures, she was enthralled. Going to the pet store was like going to the zoo, except in the pet store the clerks would actually let you cuddle an animal if you wanted to.

Jeremy obviously didn't feel the same love for pet stores. They practically had to pull him into the shop, so Meredith led him first to the parrot display where five or six parrots sat on tall perches made of vinyl piping.

"Do you like birds?" she asked simply.

"Yeah," Jeremy said, watching the birds flap their wings. "Birds are no problem. I've always liked birds."

Meredith caught Nicki's eye and nodded, and Nicki knew she was saying, *Okay. Step One. He likes birds.*

They moved next to the aquariums where thousands

of fish darted through greenery and ceramic figurines. "Aren't they nice?" Christine asked. "Don't they make you feel *relaxed*?"

"Yeah," Jeremy answered. "Fish are cool."

Next they moved to a set of aquariums where the pet store owner kept squirmier animals for sale: two tarantulas, a python and an assortment of mice, rats and gerbils.

"Ugh," Laura said, hiding her face behind her hands. "Tell me when this part is over."

"Okay, Jeremy," Scott knelt beside a display of gerbils. "Any problem with any of these animals?"

Jeremy bent down and peered into each cage. "No problem," he said simply, shrugging his shoulders.

"Okay, then," Nicki said, leading the group to the large glass window where the puppies were kept. Behind the window were several small cages and in each cage was a different breed of puppy.

"Just stand here and look at these darling puppies," Nicki said, pulling Jeremy in front of the window. "Aren't they the cutest things you've ever seen?"

Jeremy stiffened, but he stood in front of the window without flinching. "Here's a baby beagle," Christine said, lightly tapping the glass. "He will be a super hunting dog. And here's a corgi. Did you know the Queen of England raises corgis? She does. And here's a Chinese pug. Remember the movie *Milo and Otis*? Otis was a pug, just like this little guy."

Jeremy nodded and kept watching, fascinated by the little puppies. He even laughed when the pug watched him. "Hey, dude," Jeremy said softly, and the pug tilted his head as if to say, "Who, me?"

"Can I help you?" The girl who worked in the pet store

walked toward Nicki and her friends. "Is someone thinking about getting a puppy? We have some great puppy training aids for sale, too. Puppy chews, doggie beds, a puppy playpen, even dog repellant."

"Dog repellant?" Christine asked, crinkling her nose. "What's that?"

The salesgirl smiled and picked up a large aerosol can. "It's used in housebreaking puppies. They hate the smell, so you just spray it wherever you don't want them to, you know, widdle waddle or peedle poodle."

She sprayed a whiff into the air and Laura sniffed it appreciatively. "Smells nice," she said. "Like the lawn on mowing day. I don't know why dogs wouldn't like this."

The girl put the top back on the can. "I don't know either, but they don't."

"Well, we're just looking today," Nicki explained. "But do you think you could bring a puppy out for us?"

The girl shrugged. "Sure. The dogs could use the exercise. Which one do you want to see?"

"The Pekingese."

"The pug."

"The beagle."

"The shepherd."

They all gave their answers at once, and Nicki laughed. "Jeremy," she said, "which puppy would you like to see up close?"

Jeremy seemed to grit his teeth, but he finally answered, "I think maybe the poodle."

Nicki understood why Jeremy wanted the poodle. It

was a poodle that had literally run him off the track at the meet.

"Okay, the poodle," the girl said, and she ducked behind the glass window and pulled a tiny and shy poodle out of his cage.

She was about to hand the dog to Jeremy, but Christine put out her hands first. "Slowly," she said, more to the dog than to Jeremy. "We'll do this slowly."

She let the dog sit on her upturned palms and put them next to Jeremy's chest. "Try petting the dog," she suggested.

Five other pairs of hands went out immediately, but Christine laughed and held the dog closer to Jeremy. "This is for Jeremy, not for all of you," she teased, and Jeremy, surrounded by his friends, put out a tentative finger and lightly stroked the dog's head.

"He won't hurt you," Meredith said, crooning softly to the puppy.

"Would you like to hold him?" Nicki asked Jeremy.

"No," Jeremy took a step backward and shook his head. "Not today."

"Okay," Nicki said. "I think we've made some good progress. We'll work on more later."

Jeremy breathed a sigh of relief once they stepped out of the pet store. "I'm glad that's over," he said. "Now I've got to run and get at least three miles in before dinner. I'll be late getting home as it is."

"We can give you a ride," Christine offered, opening the door to the limo.

"No, thanks, I'd rather run," Jeremy said.

Scott grinned at Nicki. "I think I'll run home, too," he said. "See you tomorrow."

The boys sprinted away, and the girls got into the car. "I think Jeremy's going to be okay," Christine said as they settled back into the limo's luxurious seats. "He's forgotten about that crazy letter and he's getting used to dogs. He'll be fine in his race."

"Maybe," Nicki said, replaying the days' events in her mind. "I certainly hope so."

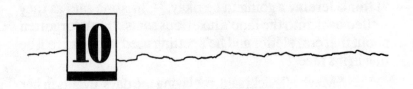

10

It was eleven-thirty according to her digital clock when Nicki felt someone shaking her shoulder. "Nicki, honey, you've got a phone call," her mother said. "It's Meredith."

"Meredith?" Nicki sat up and tried to shake the groggy feeling in her head.

"She said it was an emergency, and I hope it is," Mrs. Holland said, turning on the light. "I don't like waking you up in the middle of a school night. Try not to make it a habit."

Nicki left her room and padded down the hall to the kitchen. She picked up the phone: "Meredith?"

"Nicki, Jeremy just called me. He's even more shook up than before."

"What happened?"

"Someone called him at about eleven o'clock. When he picked up the phone, there was no sound except that of a dog growling. For a second, Jeremy thought some dog called to threaten him!"

"That's crazy!"

"That's what I thought. But Jeremy was asleep, and when he answered the phone — well, you know how weird things can seem at night."

"Are you sure he wasn't dreaming?"

"Good try, Nicki, but he was awake. He says it was a real dog, barking and growling at him on the phone."

"So—" Nicki found it hard to think straight. She was just too tired to put things together. "So what does this mean?"

"It means whoever sent the letter hasn't given up, that's what it means," Meredith answered. "Honestly, Nicki, are you awake?"

"Sort of," Nicki muttered. "Okay. Did you get Jeremy calmed down?"

"Sort of," Meredith answered.

"Then we'll talk about it tomorrow," Nicki said. "But thanks for calling."

"Okay," Meredith said. "See you in the morning."

Before school the next morning, the girls waited on the benches by the lockers for Jeremy. They finally spied him walking slowly down the hall—with Elinore Anderson right behind him. They both looked upset.

"Hey, Jeremy," Meredith called, waving to get his attention. "We're over here. Got a minute to talk?"

He looked at the girls, startled, then looked around to see if anyone else was listening. Elinore took the hint and left. Jeremy walked toward the girls, shaking his head.

"I think it's all your fault, that's what I think," he said, slowly. "None of this would be happening if you girls weren't hanging around all the time. Everybody notices. You've been asking questions and snooping around and everybody in school knows that the great mystery solvers think I'm a nut case or something. Why don't you just leave me alone?"

Nicki felt Meredith elbow her in the side. "Pssst," Meredith said, ignoring Jeremy's tirade. "Look at Elinore Anderson."

Elinore hadn't gone far. She was leaning against a nearby wall with a smug, satisfied expression on her face. For some reason, she seemed absolutely delighted that Jeremy was angry with Nicki and her friends.

"What do you make of that?" Meredith whispered, nodding toward Elinore.

"I don't know," Nicki whispered back. "But we've got to stop Jeremy. He's too upset to think straight."

Christine was way ahead of them. While Jeremy went on, she simply stood up, walked behind him, and with one movement she gently kicked his knees out from under his lanky frame.

"Ouch!" Jeremy yelped, falling forward awkwardly. "What'd ya do that for? What if I'm hurt?"

"You're not hurt," Christine said simply, returning to her seat on the bench. "But now you'll stop talking and listen, won't you? It works with my brothers every time."

"Jeremy, you're upset," Meredith said. "Why don't you sit down and quietly explain to the other girls what happened last night."

"You're the one who's causing a scene," Laura said, looking around. "If you'll just sit down and hush up, no one will think anything about you."

Jeremy did sit down on a bench and rubbed his knees. "Last night at about eleven o'clock my phone rang," he began.

"You have your own phone?" Christine asked, her eyes wide. "Lucky you."

"It's the extension in my room," Jeremy explained. "Anyway, I picked it up."

"On the first ring?" Nicki asked. "Or did it ring a while?"

Jeremy thought a minute. "I picked it up right away. I thought it might be Scott and I didn't want him to bother my parents."

"Okay, tell us what happened next," Meredith encouraged him.

"Nothing," Jeremy frowned. "I said, 'hello' and there was silence. I was about to hang up, but I heard this growling sound. It got louder and then there was barking, then growling, then snarling, and so I just hung up."

"Wow!" Christine's eyes glowed with excitement. "That's absolutely *wild*! Whoever would do that is just crazy!"

Kim was more sympathetic. "I am sorry, Jeremy," she said softly. Her small hand went out and gently touched his arm. "I am very sorry it upset you."

Jeremy ducked his head and blushed, and Kim withdrew her hand quickly. "That's not all," Jeremy said, looking up at Nicki. "It happened again this morning at about six-thirty. I was up, getting ready for school, and the phone rang. My parents were busy, so I answered it."

"Was it just the same?" Meredith asked. "No human voice?"

Jeremy nodded. "Just the same, but it didn't seem quite as spooky in the morning as it did in the middle of the night. But it was creepy. I looked around in the yard just to make sure nothing was out there before I walked to the bus stop."

"Okay," Nicki's mind was racing. "Is your family's phone number listed in the phone book?"

Jeremy nodded. "We're the only Newkirks in Pine Grove."

"So getting the phone number was easy," Meredith pointed out. "Anyone could have done it."

"Anyone with motive and opportunity," Kim added.

"Jeremy, what do you think this person is trying to say to you?" Nicki asked. "Do you think this person is trying to get you out of the five-mile race? Or are they mad at you for something?"

Jeremy put his hands around his head and leaned on his long arms. "I think they're trying to drive me crazy, that's all. And they're doing a good job of it, too."

As Meredith asked Jeremy more questions about his mysterious phone calls, Nicki looked around to see if Elinore Anderson was still lingering near. She was, and her expression wasn't nearly as smug as it had been when Jeremy was angry with the girls — now Elinore looked really upset. She was watching Jeremy as he talked to Meredith, and once when Kim leaned over to pat Jeremy's arm in sympathy, Nicki saw Elinore start forward and drop her jaw in amazement. Then she snapped her mouth shut, turned on her heel and walked off in a hurry.

"Thanks, Jeremy, for your time," Nicki said abruptly, turning back to her friends on the benches. "I think we've got what we need to know for now. We'll talk to you later."

"Sure." Jeremy shrugged and stood up, but before he left he smiled down at Kim. "See you later, okay?"

Kim cupped her face in her hands and beamed at him. "Okay."

"Oooo, what's this?" Christine teased when Jeremy had left. "Kim and Jeremy sitting in a tree, K-i-s-s-i-n-g."

"What is that poem?" Kim's expression was blank.

"Nothing," Meredith shot Christine an exasperated look. "Can we get to work on this now?"

"This is really wild," Laura said. "Who'd put a dog

up to the phone to call Jeremy? And how would he get the dog to growl at the phone? That wouldn't be easy."

"For heaven's sake, it's not a real dog," Meredith said, hitting Laura over the head with a folder. "It's a tape of a dog barking. The caller could have made the tape from anything."

"A real dog," Kim said.

"Or a sound effects tape," Christine pointed out.

"Or even a TV show," Nicki added. "It wouldn't be hard to tape a dog growling if you knew what you were looking for."

"Oh," Laura said weakly. "I didn't think of that."

"What's worse, this person can call Jeremy any time and just play that tape," Nicki said. "Jeremy will be a fruit loop if this keeps up until the big race."

"So what do we do?" Kim asked. "We have to help him. He is such a nice boy."

Nicki grinned at Kim. Apparently Kim and Jeremy had become *really* good friends. "Well, we know the person isn't finished with Jeremy," Nicki pointed out. "First, he or she sent the letter. And when that didn't work, our mystery person started making phone calls."

"Could this person have had anything to do with the dog at the park?" Christine asked. "That was really terrible."

"I doubt it," Meredith said. "I think that was just a really weird coincidence. If it had happened to any of us, we would have forgotten all about it by now. But it made a big impression on Jeremy because of his cynophobia."

"I'll bet his horoscope could have predicted it," Laura said, nodding wisely. "I'll have to ask him what his sign is."

"Get off it, Laura," Christine said, giving her friend a

harsh look. "I told you that stuff is wrong. You started out just having fun with it, but now it's really getting to you."

"It is not," Laura snapped. "But what harm could it do?"

"We don't have time to get into this now," Nicki said. "The bell rings for first period in five minutes and we might as well jump in today and interview our first suspect."

"Who?" the others asked.

Nicki winked at Laura. "Let's go with the jealous girlfriend theory. I watched Elinore Anderson this morning, and she looked really happy when Jeremy was yelling at us. But when he sat down next to Kim —" she paused and smiled at Kim, " — then Elinore seemed to get angry. We might as well start with her."

"What do we do?" Laura asked. "I love this part."

"Well, we know she has a motive," Nicki said.

"Jealousy," Laura added, nodding.

"So let's see if she's had the opportunity," Nicki said. "Could she have sent the letter? Could she have made the phone calls? Does her family subscribe to *Newsweek*? What time does she get up in the morning?" Nicki looked around her circle of friends. "Who wants to interview Elinore?"

Kim timidly raised a hand. "I am in a class with her, so I could do it."

Nicki thought a moment. "That may not be such a good idea," she said slowly. "Jeremy likes you, Kim, and Elinore's probably jealous of you now. She may not want to talk to you, and if she does, she may not tell you the truth."

"I could talk to her," Christine said, snapping her gum. "It's no big deal."

"Okay." Nicki leaned back and picked up her books.

"We'll meet at lunch and find out how it went, okay? In the meantime, someone ought to keep an eye out for D. N. Downin, too. He's next on the list of suspects."

"I will," Meredith nodded. "With pleasure."

The girls were surprised when Christine approached their lunch table with Elinore at her side. "Move your books, please, Meredith," Christine said, placing her tray on the table. "Elinore wants to eat lunch with us today."

"She does?" Nicki asked, surprised. Then she caught herself. "Oh, she does! How are you, Elinore?"

"Fine," Elinore said, shifting her tray awkwardly from one hand to the other. "I usually just eat by myself, but Christine said you all wanted me to eat with you today."

"Yes, we do," Meredith said, sliding her books off the table to make room for Elinore. "Have a seat."

Elinore Anderson seemed to be painfully shy around the older girls. She placed her tray on the table uncertainly, then wrestled her chair from beneath the table and plopped down on the seat. Underneath her too-long bangs, dark eyes peeked out like naughty children behind a curtain.

The other girls watched in silence as Elinore struggled to open a stubborn milk carton. "Try the other side," Meredith suggested finally. "The side that says, 'Open This End.' "

Elinore didn't even have the sense to be embarrassed. She just turned the milk carton around and fumbled with it again. Finally, it opened.

"Elinore was telling me about Jeremy Newkirk," Christine said, a little too casually. "They live on the same street in the Georgetown subdivision."

"There are some *lovely* homes over there," Laura gushed. "How nice for you."

Elinore sipped her milk and nodded.

"Elinore's on the track team, too," Christine said. "She runs the dash right now, but she wants to go out for the hurdles."

"I have long legs," Elinore said, crinkling her nose and laughing. "They have to be good for something, right?"

The other girls laughed agreeably, and Nicki kicked Christine under the table. *Why didn't she get to the point?*

"Uh, what do you like to read, Elinore?" Christine asked. "Have you ever read *Newsweek?*"

"Way to be subtle," Meredith muttered under her breath.

"Uh, what's that?" Elinore said, mumbling through a bite of a peanut-butter-and-jelly sandwich. "Is it a newspaper?"

"Can she really be that dumb?" Laura whispered to Nicki.

"That's not dumb," Nicki whispered back. "I mean, if you've never seen *Newsweek*, that's not a dumb question at all."

"Do you have any pets, Elinore?" Christine asked. "A dog, maybe?"

"No, we can't afford to have a dog," Elinore said, her cheeks turning pink. "My mom says she can't afford dog food. But I do have a goldfish. I got him for Christmas last year."

"Goldfish are nice," Nicki said, feeling sorry for Elinore.

"That's what Jeremy says," Elinore answered. "Jeremy named him for me. We call him King Midas, because he's gold. You know, the story about the Midas touch? Anyway, Jeremy told me about it one day when he walked me home from track practice. Jeremy's a good runner, don't you think? He runs every afternoon on our street, sometimes up and down three or four times. I told him he should run on some of the other streets too, and he laughed and said he ran on all of them but Logan Lane. I wonder why he won't run on Logan Lane? Anyway, he's the best runner in the world, I think. I know he's the best runner in the county and I can't wait for him to win that five-mile race next weekend. Then everybody will know how good he is."

Elinore ran out of breath and stopped talking. The other girls were speechless. The shy girl had trouble stringing five words together unless she was talking about Jeremy Newkirk. And she seemed to want him to win the five-mile race. She was proud of him, and in her strange way, she really adored him.

"I think," Nicki whispered to Meredith, who was sitting closest to her, "I think we can scratch this suspect off our list."

Meredith nodded in agreement. "This girl would walk through fire for Jeremy Newkirk," she whispered back. "Unless she's lying through her teeth, I don't think she's the one who's trying to scare him to death."

12

Interrogating D. N. Downin wasn't going to be so easy. First of all, he was an eighth-grader, and at school there was sort of an unbridgeable gap between the seventh and eighth graders. It also didn't help that he was a loner. He seemed nice enough, but he was intensely into running. When he wasn't in class, he was usually in the gym or out on the track, running laps. He wasn't the type to sit still for small talk.

Nicki and her friends had planned to meet after school to try to think of a way to talk to D. N., but those plans were forgotten when Jeremy Newkirk walked up to them and threw his notebook against the lockers.

The girls were startled. "What's wrong?" Nicki asked.

"Only this," Jeremy said, handing her a sheet of paper. "It's the map for the race. I was supposed to get it yesterday, but I left practice early, remember?"

Nicki looked at the map. The five-mile race apparently was supposed to start at Clearwater Middle School, wind through several neighborhoods and end at the entrance to the parking lot of Pine Grove Middle School.

"Why, look, it goes right through your neighborhood, Jeremy," Meredith said, pointing to the map with her finger. "Your parents will be able to watch the race from your driveway."

"That's not my street, that's Logan Lane," Jeremy snapped. "And I can't run in that race, not now."

"Why not?" Nicki asked, puzzled. She turned the map sideways in the hope she'd see what was upsetting Jeremy. "Has something else happened?"

"It's everything," Jeremy moaned. "I'm beginning to feel like I'm cursed or something. First there was that horrible track meet on the thirteenth. Then I get that letter. Then that dog goes berserk at the park and nearly attacks me. Then I get doggie phone calls in the middle of the night. And now this — I'm supposed to run on Logan Lane."

"What's wrong with Logan Lane?" Christine asked, crinkling her nose. "Is that where Elinore lives?"

"No, it's where Killer lives," Jeremy said. "I told you about him. He lives in the last house. Behind the wooden fence."

"Who's Killer?" Nicki asked softly.

"A pit bull dog," Jeremy said, looking off into the distance. "The meanest, roughest dog you've ever seen."

"Jeremy, this is ridiculous," Nicki said, slamming her locker shut. "You're going to be fine. Just walk with us to the park and we'll explain how we're going to take care of it."

As they started out the school doors, Nicki really had no idea what they could do to ensure that Jeremy wouldn't have a panic attack as he passed Killer's house on Logan Lane. But something had to be done. They had already worked too hard to have Jeremy drop out of the race now. But how in the world had the coaches managed to map out a race on the one street with a killer pit bull?

"It's really simple," Meredith said for the tenth time as the girls and Jeremy talked at Pine Grove Park. "You're supposed to practice on the race course this week, aren't you?

I'll run with you on Logan Lane, and we'll go by Killer's house slowly. I'll even go up to the door and ask Killer's owner to make sure the dog stays in the yard while you're running."

"Killer gets out sometimes," Jeremy said dully. "Last year he got out and the electric meter reader had to have forty stitches. It was only because Mr. Wilson promised to keep the dog chained up that they didn't put him to sleep."

"So he's chained up, right?" Christine said. "He can't get out."

"The way my luck's been going, I wouldn't bet on it," Jeremy answered. "How do I know someone wouldn't *let* him out?"

"That's ridiculous," Meredith said. "Whoever's been sending you these notes probably doesn't even know about Killer. You only know about him because you live in that neighborhood. If everyone knew, they'd be just as scared of him as you are."

"I would be careful if I was running near a pit bull dog," Kim admitted. "I have heard some awful stories about them."

"Okay, then here's what we'll do," Nicki said. "Meredith, you practice running with Jeremy. Stop by Killer's house and talk to the owner. Make sure he knows about the race and plans to keep his dog behind the fence or in the house."

"Okay," Meredith said, grinning. "Good thing I wore my sneakers."

Jeremy and Meredith walked off to do some stretching exercises before setting out on their run. Nicki and the other girls huddled together to talk, but Laura kept glancing over her shoulder.

"Now we need someone to try to talk to D. N. Downin," Nicki said. "Any volunteers?"

"I talked to Elinore," Christine grumbled. "It's someone else's turn."

Laura glanced over her shoulder again, then her face lit up like a covergirl's. "I'd love to help, but here comes Aaron," she said, dimpling. "I promised I'd meet him here at the park today. He wasn't sure he'd make it, but here he is!"

Laura hurried away to meet Aaron, and Kim smiled shyly. "I guess it is up to me," she said. "Though I do not know what to say to D. N. Downin."

"Just be yourself," Nicki said. "And find out what he thinks about Jeremy."

D. N. was jogging around the fitness trail, and Kim cut across the field to intercept him. Nicki and Christine watched her go.

"Do you think she can do it?" Christine asked. "She's so shy."

"She can probably talk to him better than anyone," Nicki said. "But we won't know for sure until later."

13

T hat's the last time I'm running with Jeremy unless you guys come along, too," Meredith announced Wednesday morning at school. "He ran circles around me. I took every short cut I could just to keep up with him, but I'm no distance runner."

"Now you see why I refuse to run," Laura said, tossing her hair back over her shoulder. "It's unfeminine to go out there and get hot and sweaty. I can't see why anyone does it."

Nicki laughed. "How long did it take you anyway, Meredith?" she asked.

Meredith raised an eyebrow. "Jeremy ran the five miles in about thirty-six minutes," she said. "He really did well until we got to Logan Lane. Then he tensed up and ran right past Killer's house without looking. I didn't get a chance to stop and talk to the owner. I was doing all I could to keep up with Jeremy."

"Maybe we should walk over there after school and talk to Killer's owner ourselves," Christine suggested. "Surely he'll listen to all five of us."

"Four of you," Laura corrected her. "I'm meeting Aaron today again at the park."

"You two are getting pretty tight, aren't you?" Meredith asked, looking suspiciously at her friend. "I thought he was supposed to be spending all his time in training for the big race."

"He is," Laura replied breezily. "We only talk for about twenty minutes or so, then he takes off to do his running. But, oh, those twenty minutes are wonderful! He really listens to me. He's sooooo nice."

Meredith's brows rushed together the way they did when she was thinking. "What do you talk about?" she asked abruptly.

"Oh, things," Laura shrugged. "School and our friends and people we know. That's all. He says he likes hearing me talk." She blushed. "He said he even likes my accent."

"Well, that's true love," Christine cracked. "Anyone who can put up with Laura's southern accent is a real gem."

Nicki looked at Kim. "I nearly forgot, Kim. Did you learn anything from D. N. Downin yesterday?"

Kim shook her head regretfully. "He does not like to talk much," she said. "He said he did not have time to talk because he had to train for the big race. I was afraid to ask him anything."

"That's okay," Meredith told Kim. "We'll talk to him later. There's another track meet tomorrow after school. Maybe we can catch D. N. there."

"Great idea." Nicki looked into her locker at the stacks of school books. She groaned. "I guess we had better get to class."

"I have an idea," Christine said, her green eyes glowing. "Why don't we walk to Sweet Eats after our talk with Killer's owner and have a banana split or something? It's been a long time since we did anything for fun."

"Yeah, we wouldn't want to work too hard," Meredith

said, smiling. "It sounds good to me. I have some extra money."

"Oh, that sounds like fun," Laura said, pausing to think. "Maybe I can walk over from the park and meet you guys there. Okay?"

"Okay," Nicki nodded. "We'll probably be there around four o'clock."

Christine grinned happily. "My mother will kill me for eating a banana split before dinner," she said. "But it'll be worth it."

Coach Linton wanted his athletes to practice at school the day before their meet with Tarpon Heights, so Jeremy pulled Kim aside and told her he wouldn't see her again until the next morning.

"That is okay," Kim said, smiling. "We girls are meeting at Sweet Eats for banana splits after our work this afternoon."

"Maybe I can meet you there, too," Jeremy said. "I'll see what I can do."

"That would be nice," Kim said, shyly looking down at the floor.

Jeremy ran off to the gym to dress for practice, and Laura stepped out from behind the lockers next to Kim. "Now wasn't that sweet," she said, putting an arm around Kim's shoulders. "Jeremy's meeting you at Sweet Eats and Aaron's meeting me at the park. Isn't life wonderful?"

Kim rolled her eyes, but Laura was staring dreamily off into the distance and didn't see. "Life is wonderful," Kim said, gathering her books and closing her locker, "but not just because I have a friend who is a boy. Boys are not all there is to life."

"Maybe not," Laura added wistfully, hugging her books to her. "But they sure add a lot of spice."

"It's this house right here," Meredith said, pointing to a small brick house with two pillars that just barely supported a sagging porch roof. "Is there a name on the mailbox?" Nicki asked, peering at the house.

"Nichols," Christine said. "That's the man's name."

The girls drew a deep breath and stepped onto the cement walkway that led up to the house. A tall wooden fence began at the front edge of the house and continued into the back yard. If there was a killer in the back yard, he was safely hidden by the fence.

"Let's go," Nicki said. They walked up the sidewalk, stepped onto the porch and rang the doorbell.

There was no answer right away. "Maybe the bell doesn't work," Meredith said. "Try knocking."

Nicki rapped lightly on the screen door, but again, there was no answer. "You're going to have to really bang on it," Christine said. "Maybe he's in the back."

"Maybe I should open the screen door and knock on the real door," Nicki said. She put her hand on the tattered screen door and pulled it open. The door squeaked in protest.

Suddenly a low, ominous growl seemed to surround the girls. "Where's that coming from?" Nicki asked, not daring to move. "Somebody, look, please!"

"He's in the window," Christine said, stiffly stepping back. "Killer's in the window, and he doesn't look happy!"

Nicki slowly let go of the screen door and let it bang back into place. Only a thin sheet of window screen separated her from a snarling, vicious dog.

"Move slowly, everyone," Meredith ordered. "Lower your eyes. Don't look at the dog. It's a sign of submission to look down at the ground, so don't look him in the eye!"

"I'm submitting," Christine said, ducking her head. "Brother, am I ever submitting!"

"Now let's slowly back up and get out of here," Meredith said quietly. "Whatever you do, don't run."

The girls were slowly inching off the porch when someone inside said, "Down, Killer!" and the dog's leering snarl left the window. A moment later, the front door opened.

"Can I help you ladies?" a raspy voice asked. "I don't want to buy nothing."

"We're not selling anything," Nicki said, raising her eyes slowly. A bald man in an undershirt and suspenders was standing on the porch.

"Mr. Nichols, we're students at Pine Grove Middle School," Meredith said. "And there's a big race this Saturday."

"So?" the man asked. "I don't want to buy a ticket."

"You don't have to," Christine said, smiling her most charming smile. "The race is being run down this street. You can sit right here in your front yard and watch the whole thing. For free."

A glint of interest sparked in the man's eye. "Really?"

"Yes, but there's one problem," Nicki said. "Killer."

"How's my dog a problem?" the man asked, crossing his arms. "He ain't hurt nobody in a long time."

"Well, one of the guys in the race knows about your dog, and frankly, he's scared to death of him," Meredith said. "So since we're friends of his, we promised we'd come by and ask you to keep Killer safely put away during the race."

"Killer's always safely put away," Mr. Nichols muttered. "Unless you're somewhere where you have no business bein.' That's what Killer's here for."

"Okay," Nicki said, feeling the conversation wasn't going at all well. "We just wanted you to know about the race. And maybe it would be a good idea to keep Killer put away out of sight because — " she had a sudden idea, " — because I'm sure you wouldn't want anyone to steal that fine dog of yours. He's a wonderful guard dog, and you know how valuable those dogs are."

Mr. Nichols's eyes narrowed. "Mebbe you've got a point there, young lady," he said. "Wouldn't hurt to keep Killer away from the windows, now, would it?"

"No," Meredith breathed a sigh of relief. "Maybe you should keep him away from the windows all week. People are going to be running by here to practice, too."

"All right." Mr. Nichols nodded and turned to go back into his house. "Thank you ladies for coming by," he said, then he slipped into the house and Nicki heard the door latch.

"Whew," she said, turning slowly to walk away. "I don't blame Jeremy for being scared of this house. I thought for a minute that Killer was going to come right out of that window after us!"

"He could," Meredith answered, glancing over her shoulder to make sure the dog was nowhere in sight. "Those dogs are very defensive of their territory. In his eyes, we were intruding on his property."

"I know just what we need now," Christine said,

laughing in relief. "One banana split, with chocolate mint chip, peanut butter and bubble gum ice cream. With marshmallow topping, hot fudge sauce, whipped cream, nuts and loads of cherries!"

"Last one to the village is Killer's breakfast," Meredith called, starting to run. "Good thing I wore my sneakers!"

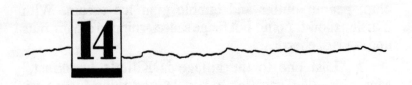

14

The girls each ordered their favorite ice cream creation and settled into a big booth at the back of the Sweet Eats shop to wait for Laura and Jeremy.

"You know, something hit me the other day," Meredith said, spooning whipped cream off the top of her ice cream. "We never asked Jeremy if he knows *why* he has cynophobia."

"You mean why is he afraid of dogs?" Christine asked. "I thought you didn't have to have a reason to have a phobia."

"Maybe," Meredith answered. "But maybe he has a reason. If we knew what it was, we could help him get over it. A phobia is an irrational fear. If Jeremy has a rational reason behind his fear, then it's not a phobia."

The bells on the Sweet Eats door jangled as Laura came in. "Hi, ya'll," Laura called, walking over to the girls with her arms full of packages. "While I waited for you to get here, I went shopping next door. I found some absolutely darling little things."

The bells jangled again, and Jeremy Newkirk came in then, all hot and sweaty. Laura made a face, but Kim smiled and slid over so he could sit in the booth next to her.

"Ugh, didn't you have time to shower?" Laura asked, raising her nose slightly.

"No," Jeremy shrugged. "There aren't any showers on the street, you know. I've just finished running six miles."

"That's good," Nicki said, but she wanted to get down to business. "Jeremy, Meredith had an idea. Do you know *why* you're afraid of dogs? Can you think of a reason? Have you always felt this way?"

Jeremy closed his eyes and shook his head. "We've never had a dog, so I'm not really used to them," he said. "My mom says when I was really little, maybe only a year old, a dog tried teething on my leg. I was in a playpen with my leg sticking out, and I didn't know how to pull it away, so the dog chewed on me for a while, I guess."

Jeremy shrugged. "I don't remember it, but I've still got the scars on my leg." To prove it, he lifted his skinny right leg onto the edge of the table. Nicki could see white lines running around his leg, like it had been tangled in barbed wire.

"Put that sweaty, hairy leg down," Laura hissed. "I've just lost my appetite."

"It's okay, Jeremy," Nicki laughed. "Laura just isn't used to sweat."

A pay phone on the wall near their booth began to ring, and the girls looked at each other.

"Should we answer it?" Christine asked.

"It's probably a wrong number," Meredith said. "We're the only ones in here."

The phone kept ringing.

"I saw this movie once where a kidnapper had the kid's father call him on a pay phone," Christine said. "So the call couldn't be traced, you know."

The phone kept ringing. "Well, I can't stand this,"

Laura said, getting up in a huff. "Someone's got to answer the thing." She picked up the phone: "Hello?"

She listened, then put the phone to her shoulder. "It's some girl asking for Jeremy Newkirk," she said. She held out the phone to Jeremy.

"What?" Jeremy gave the girls a puzzled look, but he got up and picked up the phone. "Hello?"

As he listened, his eyes widened. Nicki and Meredith sprang out of the booth and pried the telephone receiver out of Jeremy's hand. Coming through the phone was the snarling, growling, blood-thirsty yowling of a mad dog.

Nicki slammed the phone back into its cradle. "That does it!" she snapped. "Who is doing this? How did they know we'd be here? How can this person stay one step ahead of us, for heaven's sake?"

"It was a girl's voice who asked for Jeremy," Laura insisted. "It had to be Elinore Anderson."

"I really do not think it could be Elinore," Kim said. "She does not want to hurt Jeremy."

"Who else could it be, then?" Christine asked, then she snapped her fingers. "Corrin Burns!"

Nicki tilted her head. "Corrin hasn't said or done anything to Jeremy since the day after the last track meet," she pointed out. "If she's doing this, she has some crazy reason that goes beyond just being mad about the track meet."

"You never know about Corrin," Meredith pointed out. "She's done some really crazy things before."

"It was more than just a dog," Jeremy said slowly. "Before the growling started, the girl said something."

"What did she say?" Meredith asked.

"Did you recognize the voice?" Nicki asked.

Jeremy shook his head. "I didn't recognize the voice. She said, 'Killer's waiting for you on Saturday.' That's all she said."

Nicki sank back into the booth, lost in thought. How did the mystery person know about Killer? Could Mr. Nichols have something to do with this? Did he have a wife? A daughter? Was Corrin Burns somehow tied up in it all?

The girls were no closer to solving the mystery on Thursday at the next track meet. Jeremy, D. N., Scott, Elinore and all the others on the track team were determined to beat Tarpon Heights to make up for their humiliating loss to Clearwater the week before.

As she watched in the stands, Nicki felt too tired to root for the Pine Grove Panthers. This had been an unusual mystery. It was as though their mystery person had some sort of supernatural information. He or she always knew everything that was happening, and Nicki hadn't the faintest idea how to stop whatever would happen next.

She noticed Elinore Anderson down on the track, preparing to run in a girls' race. Corrin Burns was sitting down on the bleachers, but she was paying more attention to Jeff Jordan than she was to the events on the field. *Maybe Jeff put Corrin up to making that phone call,* Nicki thought. *Maybe Jeff has something against Jeremy that we don't know about.*

Nicki made a mental note to ask her friends about Corrin and Jeff, then she listened to the announcer who welcomed the crowd over the scratchy public address system. Everyone stood for the playing of the national anthem, then the crowd settled down to watch the track competition unfold.

The first event was the boys' 100-yard dash, which featured D. N. Downin and Jeremy Newkirk. Nicki watched as the boys knelt in their starting positions and the announcer called off their names. "In the last lane, running for Pine Grove, is Jeremy Newkirk," the announcer said. There was a stir among the waiting athletes from Tarpon Heights, and suddenly Nicki realized what they were doing. They were barking! They were barking like dogs and laughing in Jeremy's direction. Even the Tarpon runners on the track lowered their heads in the starting position and barked.

With anger burning within her, Nicki shot a quick glance down the bleachers at Corrin Burns and Jeff Jordan. They were practically doubled over with laughter, struggling to catch their breath between laughs so they could bark along with the Tarpon team.

The track official ignored the commotion and fired his starter's gun. The boys were off, and as Jeremy ran, Nicki could see the expression on his face. Despair was written there, and embarrassment, and defeat. Nicki wasn't surprised when he finished last in the dash. D. N. Downin finished first.

"Don't worry, the dash isn't Jeremy's best event," Meredith said, nodding toward the others. "He's a distance runner, remember?"

"Who told them to bark?" Christine asked, voicing the question they were all wondering. "Who told them about Jeremy?"

Nicki narrowed her eyes. "It could have been anybody," she said. "But I couldn't help noticing that Corrin Burns and Jeff Jordan thought the whole thing was incredibly funny."

"Could it have been D. N.?" Kim asked. Her face was bright red, and Nicki was surprised. Kim hardly ever got angry, but she looked like she could have spit nails onto the barkers with pleasure. The barking had really upset her.

"Maybe," Meredith answered. "It did seem to throw Jeremy off a little. He's never finished last before."

"I hope they do not do it all day," Kim said, her words clipped.

"I'm sure the coach will make them stop," Nicki said.

"It won't matter if he does," Meredith pointed out. "Jeremy's just been totally humiliated. I don't know if there's any way he can come back now."

He didn't. Jeremy Newkirk finished last in his best event, the mile run, and Pine Grove lost another track meet.

"I feel so guilty about what happened to Jeremy," Laura moaned the next morning in homeroom. "I read my horoscope last night, and it said I should avoid sulking but be sure to tell my friends how I feel."

"What are you talking about?" Meredith whispered, leaning forward in her desk. "What does that have to do with Jeremy?"

"I should have asked Jeremy what his sign was and told him what it said," Laura said impatiently. "Don't you see? Maybe it would have said something like, 'Don't run in a major race,' and I could have spared him all that embarrassment."

"That's crazy," Christine said, lightly powdering her freckles. She checked her reflection in her compact, then snapped it shut. "Those horoscope things are so vague, they could apply to anybody. And you're really getting hooked, Laura, and you shouldn't be reading them at all!"

"I'm not hooked," Laura replied, turning her back on Christine. "And you can't tell me what to do, either."

Nicki sighed. Ever since she had been seeing Aaron Oakman and reading horoscopes, Laura had steadily been getting harder to live with. What was it about girls when they got boyfriends? Sometimes they turned into different people!

"I thought you were supposed to avoid sulking," Christine laughed.

Laura put her hands over her ears and put her head down on her books. Nicki decided to ignore her.

"Well, Jeremy simply has to win that race tomorrow," she said. "If he does, all those other runners from Clearwater and Tarpon Heights will stop barking at him and know what a good runner he is."

"How do we know they won't be barking tomorrow?" Christine asked.

"I doubt they will," Meredith answered. "It'll be a smaller crowd. There probably won't be many people at the starting line except for the runners. The spectators will be spaced out along the route all the way up to the finish line."

"You know, we ought to space ourselves out along the race course, too," Nicki suggested. "That way we can run along with Jeremy and keep an eye on things."

"It would especially be helpful if we positioned ourselves around Mr. Nichols' house," Meredith pointed out. "That's where Jeremy is going to need the most moral support."

"I'm up for a little jog tomorrow," Nicki said. "How 'bout you, Laura?"

"I'm not listening," Laura said, her hands still over her ears. "And I'm not jogging."

"Too bad," Meredith said, winking at Nicki. "Because I'm sure Aaron Oakman will be running, too."

Laura uncovered her ears and turned back around to face her friends. "Well, maybe I could cover the beginning of the race," she said slowly. "Then Mr. Peterson could drive me to the finish line where I could wait on him — I mean, them."

"That's great," Nicki said. "Let's find Jeremy and tell him our plan."

When the bell rang the girls walked through the halls looking for Jeremy, but he wasn't easy to find. Meredith finally spotted him sitting on a bench outside the school building.

"Hey, Jeremy," she opened a door and called outside to him. "You're going to be late for your next class."

"I don't care," he said, bending down to place his head in his hands. "I'm too sleepy to sit in class."

Meredith and Nicki walked outside and stood next to Jeremy. "Why are you so tired?" Meredith asked. "Haven't you been taking your vitamins? You have a big day tomorrow, you know."

"No, I don't think I do," Jeremy said, leaning back and squinting up at Meredith. "I don't think I'm going to run."

"What?" Nicki said. "You can't give in now! If you don't run, you're just giving in to whoever's been calling you and making your life miserable. You can't give up!"

"I got three more growling phone calls last night," Jeremy said, nodding drowsily. "I had to unplug the phone. And when I finally did go to sleep, I dreamed I was running on Logan Lane. You were there, Meredith, running with me, but suddenly you screamed and Killer came out of Mr. Nichols' fence. He came and grabbed my leg and started chewing . . . " Jeremy shuddered. "It was horrible. I woke up in a cold sweat and didn't sleep the rest of the night."

Meredith playfully slugged Jeremy's shoulder. "It was just a dream, kiddo. You've had all this on your mind, and it came out in a dream. It doesn't mean anything."

"I'm just tired," Jeremy mumbled. "Sick and tired of

the whole thing. Everybody at school laughs at me, someone's trying to drive me crazy and I can't sleep at night. My mom and dad think I did something to someone, and they're mad 'cause the phone's ringing all the time."

"It won't ring after you win that race tomorrow," Meredith said firmly. "And no one will laugh when you win the trophy for our school. But you need some rest. Maybe you should go lie down in the clinic. You don't look so good."

"I'll be okay." Jeremy stood up as the bell rang.

"Brother," Nicki groaned. "Now we're all late to class."

"We've got a good reason," Meredith said, practically pulling Jeremy into the building behind her. "We're making sure the champion of the Pine Grove Panthers is on course for tomorrow."

Nicki felt pretty good about Jeremy Newkirk until Coach Linton stopped her in the hall. "You're Nicki Holland, aren't you?" he asked, looking her over as if she were a species of insect.

"Yes," Nicki answered. "I was just on my way to get a tardy slip."

"I want to have a word with you, young lady," Coach went on, ignoring Nicki's comment. "What do you think you're doing with my track team?"

"With the track team?" Nicki was dumbfounded. "Nothing."

"You're messing with some heads," Coach said. "You've got Jeremy Newkirk jumping every time he sees a shadow. D. N. Downin says some little girl has been spying on him because you told her to. Our team is the laughingstock of every team in the county. And our girls — " he slapped the side of his head. "Elinore Anderson hasn't had a good race in four days. She keeps saying that you're trying to steal her boyfriend."

"That's not me, that's Kim," Nicki said softly. "And Kim's not stealing anybody. Jeremy just likes her, that's all."

"Well, stop it!" Coach stomped his foot. "I don't know what you're doing, young lady, but stay away from my track team. You think you can do that?"

Nicki bit her lip and didn't answer. Was she really making things worse for people? Were Elinore and D.N. and Jeremy really worse off since she began investigating the mystery?

"I won't bother anyone," she said, telling the truth as much as she could. "I was only trying to help."

"Go help someone else," Coach said, turning away. As he walked toward the gym, he kept talking to himself and flailing his arms. Nicki watched him go, a lump rising in her throat. She had never felt so stupid and so far away from finding the truth.

Nicki was unusually quiet at lunch. "Aren't we going to plan our positions for the race tomorrow?" Meredith asked her. "What's wrong, Nicki?"

Nicki shook her head. "I just wonder if we aren't doing something to make things worse," she said. "I mean, it seems like every time we do something, something worse happens to Jeremy. And maybe our asking questions has just added fuel to the fire, you know? Everybody's talking, and because of it, Jeremy's getting more and more embarrassed."

The other girls were quiet, and Nicki wondered if maybe they had thought the same thing but were too loyal to speak up.

"I just feel like we've come to a dead end," Christine said. "I mean, I really don't think Elinore did any of this. And Corrin Burns told me she's going out of town tomorrow, and she could care less who wins the five-mile race."

Just then D. N. Downin hobbled into the cafeteria on crutches. "Look behind you," Meredith told Nicki. "Look who just came in!"

D. N. made his way to a table of boys who surrounded him with questions. Nicki got up and walked over to the group, hoping to overhear what happened to D. N. Did this have anything to do with the mystery?

"How'd you do that?" Scott Spence was asking D. N. "Running?"

"No way," D. N. laughed. "I threw a karate kick at my brother."

"And he kicked you, right?"

D. N. laughed again. "I wish. I just lost my balance and fell. Something popped, I guess, and I've thrown my knee out. The doctor says it'll be good as new in about three weeks."

"So you're not running tomorrow?" Nicki's voice cut through the boy's voices, and they turned to look at her, surprised that a girl had come up to the table.

"Yeah, Nicki, I'm running like this," D. N. said sarcastically. "I'll win first place in the crutches category."

Nicki bit her lip and left. She'd forgotten that D. N. thought she was spying on him. No wonder he was so sharp with her.

She sat back down at her table. "D. N.'s out of the race," she told the other girls. "So if he's the one who wanted Jeremy out, it's all over now."

"I don't know," Meredith said thoughtfully. "D. N.'s a good sprinter, but I don't think he could have won even if Jeremy was out of the race. Clearwater's Aaron Oakman is much faster than D. N. And there are probably a couple of other distance runners who would beat D. N."

"I do not understand the difference," Kim said, "between a distance runner and a sprinter."

Meredith was happy to explain. "It's based on the kind of muscles you inherited from your parents," she said. "Distance runners have a high share of slow-twitch muscles which don't produce lactic acid. They draw on the fuel they have stored as carbohydrates. That's why distance runners eat pasta before a race."

"What about sprinters?" Christine asked.

"They have a higher share of fast-twitch fibers," Meredith explained. "They can run really fast only for about 400 yards. After that, lactic acid accumulates in their muscle tissue and slows them down."

"Absolutely fascinating," Laura said in a bored tone. "I'm glad Aaron doesn't bore me with stuff like this."

"What does he talk about?" Nicki asked, suddenly interested.

Laura giggled. "About me, mostly. About how nice I am, and how pretty, and how he likes my hair." She shrugged. "Sounds pretty silly, doesn't it?"

"And what do you talk to Aaron about?" Meredith asked, leaning forward.

"Oh, I don't know. About you all. About school. About our mysteries. I told him about all those Tarpon people barking at Jeremy, for instance, and he was really sweet. He said they shouldn't have done that because it wasn't good sportsmanship."

Suddenly a new door of understanding opened for Nicki. Things that hadn't made sense glowed in a new light of possibility.

"Okay," she said, grabbing a sheet of notebook paper. "Let's draw a map. This is really important. Laura, you're going to start and end the race with Jeremy, right?"

"With all the runners," Laura corrected her. "Aaron's running too, you know."

"I know," Nicki smiled at Laura. "So you be there when the race begins and ends and watch out for anything strange, okay?"

"Okay."

"Kim, can you meet Jeremy at the entrance of Georgetown Estates? Just run with him until the beginning of Logan Lane."

Kim nodded. "I think I can run that far." She smiled at Meredith. "I think I probably have slow-twitch muscles."

"Okay." Nicki looked at the map. "Meredith, can you meet Jeremy at the beginning of Logan Lane and run with him past Mr. Nichols' house?"

"Sure," Meredith nodded. "He really kicks into high gear when he passes Killer's house. I'll try to keep him steady."

"Good. I'm going to visit with Mr. Nichols that morning just to make sure everything's okay," Nicki said. "And Christine, can you run with Jeremy from the end of Logan Lane until the finish line?"

"Or as far as I can go," Christine said. "But if he's past Logan Lane, he should be fine, right?"

"Right," Nicki answered. She looked at her map again, then up at her friends. "I have a feeling that something's about to break loose," she said. "And tomorrow we'd better be prepared for anything."

That night after dinner, Nicki called Laura. "Hi, Laura," Nicki said. "I just wanted to tell you that you don't have to be at the starting line tomorrow if you don't want to. I think Jeremy might scratch and drop out of the race. He just doesn't seem very enthusiastic about the idea of running past Killer's house."

"That's too bad," Laura seemed genuinely sympathetic. "But I'll probably be at the race anyway, Nicki."

Nicki could hear the smile in her voice. "Aaron's running, too, you know."

"I know." Nicki forced a yawn. "Well, I'm tired. See you sometime tomorrow, I guess."

"Okay. Bye."

17

S aturday morning was hot and clear for March, and a strong, gusty wind blew Nicki's hair as she rode with her father to Clearwater Middle School, the starting point of the race.

"I know you don't always like to discuss your mysteries," her father said, driving into the parking lot, "but be careful today, okay? There are a lot of people here and you know how I feel about letting you loose into a group of strangers."

"It's okay, Dad," Nicki reassured her father. "I'll be with the other girls, too. And whatever happens, our mystery should be solved by the end of the day." She muttered under her breath as she got out of the car: "I just hope the good guy wins in the end."

There was an air of expectancy around the runners who were doing stretches on the asphalt of the parking lot. Aaron Oakman was there, in shorts and a tank top, standing with a dark-haired girl who held a windbreaker and a towel. Nicki watched them for a minute before looking around for other people she might know.

Coach Linton's van pulled into the parking lot and out piled Scott Spence, Elinore Anderson and Jeremy Newkirk. All three were dressed to run.

Scott saw Nicki and gave her a friendly wave. "Where

have you guys been?" Nicki called. "I thought they might start the race without you."

Scott jerked his thumb toward Coach Linton. "He wanted to make sure we stretched out and warmed up," he said. "So he made us do it in the gym at school."

"That makes sense," Nicki called back.

The boys made their way over to the coach, and Elinore Anderson hopped in place, her pigtails flapping rhythmically up and down.

"Elinore!" Nicki called, surprised. "I thought you weren't going to run!"

Elinore smiled happily and kept bouncing in place. "Coach signed me up anyway, and I thought it'd be fun. Who knows? With these long legs I might even win the girls' race. Jeremy thinks I might, and Jeremy should know 'cause he's the best runner in the county, don't you think so?"

"Probably," Nicki said. *Always Jeremy,* Nicki thought. At least he looked better today than he did yesterday in school. Apparently he had rested. And Nicki had to admit he looked better in runners' shorts and a tank top than he did in school clothes. A little leggy, maybe, but he looked natural.

Nicki wasn't the only one who had noticed the arrival of the Pine Grove kids. Aaron Oakman walked over and extended his hand to Jeremy. "I heard you had dropped out of the race," he said, smiling. "Glad you didn't. Good luck."

"Sure." Jeremy stopped stretching long enough to shake Aaron's hand. "Good luck to you, too."

Aaron walked away, the dark-haired girl still following. Aaron whispered something to her, and she nodded and walked toward the parking lot. *Maybe she's his sister,* Nicki thought. *Or a team trainer. Or a friend. Who knows?*

The shiny flash and collective "ahhhh" from the crowd told Nicki Laura had arrived in her limo. "Hey, Nicki," Laura said, hopping out and catching sight of her friend, "I didn't think I'd see you this morning."

"Jeremy decided to run after all," Nicki said slowly, watching Laura. "And Elinore Anderson's running, too."

Laura raised her eyebrows in surprise. "Really? I'm impressed." She looked around and caught sight of Aaron. "Aaron!" she caught his attention and waved. "Well, see you later, Nicki," she said. "Gotta go."

"See you," Nicki echoed.

Nicki walked over to Jeremy. He was sitting on the ground with one leg outstretched in front of him and the other tucked behind him. "Are you ready?" she asked.

"Yeah," he answered, bending his chest to his knee. "I talked to Meredith and she says I don't have cynophobia."

"You don't?"

"No," Jeremy said, switching legs. "I just had a bad experience once and I kept telling myself that I was afraid of dogs. But I don't have to be. Meredith says the answer is trust."

"Trust?" Nicki said. "Like you're trusting us to help you?"

"Sort of," Jeremy answered. "And I'm trusting Mr. Nichols to keep Killer in the fence. If everything else fails," he laughed, "I'm trusting God to keep me from being eaten alive."

"Sounds good to me," Nicki laughed.

A whistle blew, and the runners stopped stretching and made their way to a white chalked line across the entrance to Clearwater's parking lot. Jeremy stopped to pull up his socks and adjust the headband on his head. Aaron Oakman sprayed his legs and arms with spray from a large silver can, then handed it to Laura. He tweaked her nose, then bent down to touch his toes one final time.

The crowd grew quiet, and the starter's gun popped. The runners were off. Nicki and Laura watched as they headed out of the parking lot and down the street. Nothing drastic had happened, but Nicki couldn't get rid of the uneasy feeling in her stomach. Jeremy was trusting her—could she guarantee that everything would be all right?

Nicki walked over to Laura. "I need to borrow Mr. Peterson," she said. "Do you think he'd drop me off at Logan Lane?"

Laura was feeling generous. "Sure, Nicki," she said, all smiles. "I'll even wait with you if you want. After the runners pass there, we can go ahead to the finish line."

"Sounds great." Nicki and Laura piled into the limo, and pulled out into the sunshine, passing the runners. At the front of the pack, Nicki noticed, were two boys: Aaron Oakman and Jeremy Newkirk.

Nicki spied Kim waiting at the entrance to Georgetown Estates. Like Nicki, Kim was wearing regular shorts and a tee-shirt and sneakers with extra thick socks. Kim caught sight of the limo and gave the darkened windows a "thumbs up" sign.

"Kim's in position and ready," Nicki said, settling back. "And Meredith should be up here at the beginning of Logan Lane."

Mr. Peterson tooted the limo's horn when he saw Meredith, who smiled and waved, too. "We need to go to the brick house on the left," Nicki pointed out. "The one with the big privacy fence."

Mr. Peterson nodded and drove slowly up the street. "So, Laura," Nicki said, looking over at her friend. "How well do you know Aaron, anyway?"

Laura dimpled. "Well enough, I guess, since I've only known him a week."

"Does he have any sisters?"

Laura frowned. "I don't know. I don't think so."

"Does he have a dog?"

"I don't know."

"What do his parents do?"

Laura kept frowning. "I don't know. I guess it never came up. What are you trying to do, Nicki, prove something? If you are, it doesn't matter because my horoscope told me that true love was just around the corner. That's got to be Aaron."

"No, I'm not trying to prove anything," Nicki said, turning to look out the window. "Just curious." She paused a moment. "When you talked to Aaron last night, did you make plans for after the race?"

Laura shrugged. "I just told him I'd meet him at the finish line." Her eyes grew wide. "Hey, how'd you know I talked to him last night?"

"Just a hunch," Nicki said as the car pulled into Mr. Nichols' driveway. "Thanks, Mr. Peterson." Nicki jumped out of the car. Mr. Nichols was sitting on his lawn in a tattered lawn chair, a glass of lemonade in one hand and a *People* magazine in the other. His mouth fell open at the sight of a Rolls Royce in his driveway.

"Good morning, Mr. Nichols," Nicki said, walking slowly up the walkway. "Remember me?"

He grunted and smiled. "Yep. You were right. It's kinda excitin' to have a race comin' across my front yard." He grunted and jerked his thumb toward the car. "Am I on *Candid Camera*? Whose car is that?"

"It belongs to a friend of mine," Nicki said. "Do you mind if we sit here and watch the race for a while? We'll leave as soon as the runners pass by here."

"I don't mind," Mr. Nichols said, a sly grin growing across his face, "if you'll let me sit in that car for a while."

Mr. Peterson stepped gallantly out of the driver's seat. "You may sit behind the wheel if you like," he said in his dignified voice. "If that's all right with you, Miss Laura."

"Sure," Laura called from the back seat, sounding bored.

Mr. Nichols put down his *People* and his drink and hoisted himself out of the lawn chair. He approached the car almost reverently and eased himself behind the wheel. *There he sits,* Nicki thought, *as happy as a frog on a lily pad.*

Nicki looked around, but there were no signs of Killer. His face wasn't in the window, either. "Is Killer put away, Mr. Nichols?" Nicki called.

"Yep," Mr. Nichols said. "Safe as can be."

Nicki sat down on the curb and waited for the runners to come. Other spectators began to come out, too. People came out of their houses and parents pulled up on bicycles and motor scooters to watch this segment of the race. Kim rode up, too, on the basket of someone's bicycle, and she waved to Nicki. For a moment Nicki thought she saw the brown-haired girl who had been with Aaron, but when she looked again, she was nowhere to be found in the crowd on the street. "I think I'm imagining things," Nicki laughed to herself. "Maybe I'll be dreaming about dogs next."

The crowd applauded when Jeremy finally came into view, and Nicki breathed a sigh of relief. True to her word, Meredith had fallen into step beside him to lend moral support, and only Clearwater's Aaron Oakman was even near Jeremy. *All Jeremy has to do is pass Mr. Nichols' house without having a panic attack,* Nicki thought, *and he'll win this race!*

"Here they come!" Nicki called. Mr. Nichols squirmed his body out of the car and gave Mr. Peterson an appreciative pat on the back. "Fine machine," he said solemnly. "Mighty fine machine."

"Thank you, sir," Mr. Peterson nodded.

Mr. Nichols sat back in his lawn chair and sipped his lemonade. Jeremy and Meredith were out in front, and as they approached, Nicki could hear Meredith chanting something as she ran: "In-what-time-I-am-afraid-I-will-trust-in-God." Jeremy's lips were moving slightly, as if he were chanting, too, but Nicki knew he was saving his breath for the all-important race.

Suddenly Aaron Oakman broke into a sprint and passed Jeremy and Meredith, grinning. Nicki saw Jeremy give Meredith a puzzled look, but then there was no mistaking the snarling howl that erupted from a corner of Mr. Nichols' yard.

It was just like Jeremy's nightmare. Nicki turned and saw the gate on the tall wooden fence swing open. There was a flash of bristly fur and teeth and anger. Killer was loose, and his fangs were bared and gleaming.

He was streaking right toward Jeremy Newkirk!

18

The crowd of spectators parted like the Red Sea as Killer bore down upon the only running objects he could see: Aaron, Jeremy and Meredith. He seemed to run after Aaron for a moment, then abruptly cut in front of Jeremy and Meredith who were running right for him.

"Close your eyes and stop where you are!" Meredith shouted to Jeremy. "Trust me, Jeremy!"

Jeremy threw his head back and closed his eyes, stopping dead in his tracks. The snarling pit bull blocked his path.

"Don't look him in the eye," Meredith warned. "He'll see that as a challenge."

Nicki looked around her. Mr. Nichols wasn't even watching the race, he was staring intently at Laura's car. "Mr. Nichols!" Nicki shouted, grabbing his arm. "Your dog is out!"

Mr. Nichols looked into the street and saw Killer blocking Jeremy and Meredith's path. "What the—" he began. "How'd he get out?"

Jeremy couldn't stand the tension and ignored Meredith's command. He opened his eyes and stared at Killer in horror. Killer stopped growling and was about to lunge when suddenly a gruff voice rang out from the crowd: "Down, Killer!"

The dog lowered his tail and slunk away toward the

house. Mr. Nichols stared dumbly, surprised to hear his own voice when he hadn't said a word.

Nicki was startled for a minute, too, then she realized what had happened. "Kim!" she said, throwing her head back in delight and surprise. "Kim did it! Kim used your voice, Mr. Nichols!"

"Run, Jeremy, the race is yours," Nicki shouted. "Hurry up! You can do it!"

Jeremy sprinted away with new energy. "Adrenalin will help him catch up," Meredith said, walking toward Nicki. "That was close!"

Nicki patted the surprised Mr. Nichols on the arm. "I just don't know how that dog got out," Mr. Nichols said, shaking his head. "That gate has a good strong latch. Come here, and I'll show you."

He and Nicki walked around to the gate where Killer had slunk away, and Mr. Nichols gave it a solid push until it latched securely. "You see?" Mr. Nichols said, pointing to the latch. "I purposely put it up high so none of the neighborhood little kids could open it. And I put the latch on the outside so the dog couldn't open it. I can't for the life of me figure out how that thing opened."

"I think I can," Nicki said, looking around at the thinning crowd. "Thanks, Mr. Nichols, for your help."

Nicki, Laura, Kim and Meredith rode in the limo as they followed Jeremy and Christine on the last leg of the race.

"It looks like we aren't going to be able to catch Aaron Oakman," Meredith moaned. "And Jeremy really had him, too. If Aaron hadn't sprinted ahead at Logan Lane, and if the dog hadn't come out, Jeremy could have won easily."

"How did that dog get out?" Kim asked. "And isn't it strange that what really happened was so much like Jeremy's dream?"

"It's not strange at all when you think about it logically," Nicki said.

"What do you mean?" Meredith asked.

Nicki smiled. "I'll explain it in a minute. I need one piece of proof, though, and I think I know where to get it."

"Excuse me, ladies," Mr. Peterson interrupted. "But there's a racer down in the road. I think he's got a cramp or something in his leg."

"It isn't Jeremy, is it?" Kim asked, leaning over Meredith to look out the window.

"Oh, it's Aaron," Laura moaned as they passed him lying in the road. "What's wrong?"

Meredith tapped the window thoughtfully as she watched Christine and Jeremy easily run past Aaron. "You can get a cramp if you run too fast in the middle of the race, like Aaron did on Logan Lane," she said simply. "Or if you don't stretch out enough and warm up at the beginning of a race."

Nicki smiled. "That's what I thought. And thanks to you, Laura, Aaron didn't get much time to stretch out at the beginning of the race today."

"Why not?" Laura frowned. "I didn't stop him from doing anything."

"Oh yes, you did," Nicki said. "You'll see what I mean in a minute. Right now, I think Jeremy's about to win this race."

Mr. Peterson pulled the car to the side of the road and the girls clambered out. Christine left Jeremy's side and fell, exhausted, onto the curb. Jeremy ran on alone toward the finish line.

"He's done it," Meredith yelped. "Yea! Pine Grove wins!"

Jeremy slowed to a jog while the time keeper at the end of the line walked along beside him and shook his hand. "Congratulations, son," the man said. He handed Jeremy a tall trophy and whispered something in his ear. Jeremy smiled and put the trophy down on the ground. "Just let me catch my breath," he said, hanging his head down.

"Sure, son!" the man laughed, and clapped Jeremy on the back. "A fine race! If you keep up this good work, you'll be able to win a college scholarship. Maybe we'll even see you in the Olympics!"

Once Jeremy had regained his breath, he unlocked his long legs and walked over to where the girls were waiting.

"Congratulations!" Christine squealed. "That's a great trophy! And did they give you the $200?"

Jeremy grinned. "They're going to send it in the mail," he said. "And I know my mom will make me save it for college or something. But here's the school trophy! Now I can make up for the last two track meets I blew for them."

"It was not your fault," Kim said quietly. "No one blames you."

Jeremy smiled at her gratefully. "I didn't think I was going to make it there for a while," he panted. "But I know I couldn't have done it without all of you." He paused. "I'm glad I trusted you. I almost didn't run."

"It was nothing," Nicki said. "You won this race on your own, and against all the efforts of someone who really didn't want you in this race today."

"Who?" Jeremy was curious.

"Him," Nicki said, pointing down the road to Aaron Oakman, who was being helped off the pavement by two of his teammates.

"How can you say that?" Laura demanded indignantly. "Prove it."

Nicki nodded. "Okay, I will. Or rather, Laura, you will."

19

There were several people around Aaron Oakman, including a couple of his buddies, Clearwater's coach and the dark-haired girl Nicki had noticed earlier. But Laura ignored them all and, pushing her way toward Aaron, fell on the grass where he lay stretched out in pain.

"Are you okay?" she asked tenderly. "What happened?"

Aaron lay back on the grass, his eyes closed. "Will somebody get this goofy blonde off me?" he barked crossly. When no one moved, he raised his head and looked straight at Laura. "Leave me alone, will you? Get lost!"

Laura made a helpless squeaking sound and backed away. Nicki calmly walked over. "Aaron Oakman, you deserve to be disqualified from this race even if you didn't finish," she said in a loud, clear voice. "You've got to be the most unfair, conniving, jealous athlete in the county."

Aaron screwed his face up in pain and anger. "You can't say things like that to me," he said, closing his hands into fists. "My parents will sue you."

"No they won't," Nicki said. "Because it was you who sent Jeremy Newkirk that letter threatening him with the dog. You knew Jeremy doesn't like dogs because you saw him get scared at the track meet a week ago. I'll bet your parents subscribe to *Newsweek*, and I'll bet there's a big hole in the page with the Iron Man ad on it."

"This girl's nuts," Aaron mumbled to his friends. "Get me out of here."

"I get it," Meredith said, snapping her fingers. "You mailed that letter to Jeremy because you couldn't stick it in his locker—you don't go to our school. Then you made a tape and called his house and played it over the phone. You did this several times, even following Jeremy around town and calling him on a pay phone."

"That's insane." Aaron sat up and spat on the ground.

"It makes perfect sense to me," Christine said, kneeling next to Aaron. She waved her finger in his face. "You knew everything about Jeremy because you were using Laura to find out everything he was doing. You knew where Jeremy would be and what he was afraid of. You learned from Laura that he hated Logan Lane and that Killer lived over there. You even told someone on the Tarpon Heights team about Jeremy so they'd bark at him." Christine glared at him. "You thought that was really funny, didn't you, Aaron?"

Aaron shook his head in cold contempt. "Who do you girls think you are, Perry Mason? You're nuts, and you're wrong. What's more, you can't prove anything."

Laura was standing quietly in shocked silence. "I did tell you all that stuff," she whispered. "But I never dreamed you'd use it against me. I thought you *liked* me."

"I can prove something," Nicki said. "This morning you didn't have time to stretch out because at the last minute you found out that Jeremy was in the race after all. But he never really dropped out. I just mentioned it to Laura, thinking that she'd probably tell you. She did, and you bought it. So when Jeremy showed up, you had to move fast to take care of two things."

"Oh yeah?" Aaron's lip curled in disdain. "What?"

"First, you had to make sure someone would open Killer's gate just as the runners came by," Nicki said softly. "So you asked your real girlfriend to do it." Nicki looked up at the dark-haired girl who was standing by in the crowd. "Hi. I take it you're his girlfriend. Did you know he was seeing Laura, too?"

The girl's eyes filled with angry tears, and she shook her head. "You brat," she snapped at Aaron. "After all I did for you!" She turned and walked away.

"Just to make sure Killer wouldn't take off after you, you sprayed yourself with dog repellant," Nicki said. "I saw you do it this morning. I even saw you hand the can to Laura. You took the label off, so no one would know what you were doing."

Laura's mouth fell open. "He told me it was something runners use to keep cool," Laura said. "I still have the can in the car."

"Get it," Nicki said. Laura ran to the car and from a pocket in the interior she pulled out the silver can and sprayed a whiff into the air. "Nicki's right," she said, walking back toward the group with the can. "My nose is never wrong. It smells like the lawn after it's been mowed—just like dog repellant."

"Jeremy is the best runner in the county and you knew it," Kim said. "He was your only real competition."

"But you ruined your own race by not stretching and by bursting into that sprint on Logan Lane," Meredith added. "You didn't want to be near when Killer came out, did you?"

"Is this true, son?" Clearwater's coach had heard everything. Aaron hung his head, and the man extended his hand to Nicki. "I'm Aaron's stepdad, Coach Milton," he said.

"And now I understand," he frowned down at Aaron, "why my son insisted we map out the course along Logan Lane."

Aaron looked as if he might cry, and Nicki actually felt a little sorry for him, even after all the trouble he'd caused. Coach Milton knelt on the grass by Aaron and flattened his lips into a thin line: "Son, maybe I've been too hard on you. If I've ever made you feel that you had to win to please me, I was wrong. I'm happy if you do the best you can do, and if that means second place, then I'll be happy with second place. You don't have to cheat to be a winner in my book."

He paused and let out a big breath. "Is the leg feeling better?"

Aaron steadied his voice. "Yeah. It feels a lot better."

"Then let's go home, son."

Coach Milton stood up and held out his hand to Aaron, who grasped it and stood to his feet. Aaron paused a moment in front of Jeremy. "I'm really sorry," Aaron said. "I guess I didn't know how much it would upset you. I thought it would just spook you, you know, so you wouldn't want to run."

"Uh, that's okay," Jeremy said, looking over at Meredith. "Maybe I needed to get the spooks worked out of me anyway. I mean, today I actually came face to face with a dog that wanted to eat my face off and I didn't faint or anything. That's progress."

Aaron smiled a lop-sided grin, then moved after his father. The knot of people dispersed, and the girls and Jeremy walked to Laura's car.

Scott was waiting by the limo, panting. "Fifth place," he said, taking deep breaths. "Not bad for a high jumper."

"Hop in," Nicki said, opening the car door. "We'll take you home."

"What are ya'll getting in my car for?" Laura said as they began to pile in. "I thought ya'll were so bloomin' fond of exercise!"

"I have had my fill for today," Kim said, smiling at Jeremy. "I think it is time for a rest."

"Hey, look who won first place for the girls," Meredith said, looking toward the finish line. "Elinore Anderson!"

Elinore was carrying her trophy and standing on tiptoe searching the crowd. She spied Nicki getting into the car. "Nicki," she called. "Have you seen Jeremy?"

"Quick," Jeremy said, ducking low in the seat. "Get me out of here!" Nicki hopped in and shut the door as the girls laughed and Mr. Peterson promptly took off.

As they drove, Laura reached into her purse, pulled out a little book and tore it in half.

"What are you doing?" Nicki asked.

"It's my horoscope book," Laura said, gritting her teeth as she tore the pages into small pieces. "It said I was supposed to find the love of my life, remember? I trusted this stupid thing!"

Nicki laughed. "I guess the love of your life won't be found in a horoscope, will it?"

"That reminds me," Kim said, shyly pulling a piece of paper from her pocket. "I wrote a poem for you, Laura."

"You did?" Laura's eyes widened. "What about?"

"Shall I read it?" Kim looked around for approval. "It is not very professional."

"Sure, read it," Christine said. "We didn't know you wrote poetry."

"Sometimes," Kim said, unfolding the paper. "When I am in the mood."

She took a deep breath and began reading:

> Sometimes no matter where you go,
> Or what you try to do,
> People always want to know —
> "Hey, what sign are you?"

> My birthday really doesn't count —
> My life's not in the stars.
> They were created just like me —
> Like dogs and trees and Mars.

"I like the part about the dogs," Jeremy said, winking at Kim. "Keep going."

Kim kept reading:

> The One who created all good things
> Has a special plan for me.
> I see it as I learn and grow
> To be what He wants me to be.

> If I have a "sign" at all,
> It's the cross of Calvary.
> Jesus broke down all the walls,
> And He has set me free.

"That's really beautiful, Kim," Laura said softly. "Thanks. I know I'll never read a horoscope again." She let the little pieces of the ripped-up book fall onto the floor of the car and leaned back into the comfortable upholstery. "I'll never fall in love again, either."

"Fat chance," Christine giggled. "You'll probably fall in love again next week."

"Well, I know who I'm in love with," Jeremy said.

The girls all looked at Kim, and she blushed.

"I'm in love with that Pekingese puppy," Jeremy went on, slapping his bony knees. He leaned forward. "Can you take us to the pet store, Mr. Peterson? I'm just dying to hold that little dog."

"Sounds like a wonderful idea," Mr. Peterson said, turning the car around. "There's nothing like a puppy to make you feel good all over."

"Yes, sir," Jeremy answered. "Nothing at all."

* * * *

Don't miss what's next for Nicki, Kim, Laura, Christine and Meredith . . .

The Case of the Counterfeit Cash

Nicki and Christine swam to the stern of the boat, where the overhead light on deck threw shadows in the water. Nicki lifted her face mask. "Are you going to climb up, or should I?"

Christine's mouth fell open and her eyes bugged. "Behind you," she squealed. "Look!"

Nicki whirled around. Behind her something was rising out of the water — something big and dark and sinister, with arms like a giant sea serpent!

Nicki expected fun and sun in the summer before her eighth grade year — not mysterious strangers and counterfeit cash! The girls are warned to leave the mystery alone. But when Nicki is threatened, she has to solve the mystery to save her own life!

About the Author

Angie Hunt lives in Largo, Florida, with her husband Gary, their two children, and a Chinese pug named Ike. She and Gary have been serving in youth ministry for fourteen years. Her family lives on a canal where foxes, alligators, otters, ducks, pelicans and snakes regularly come to visit. She types out Nicki Holland novels while chewing her favorite food — extra-large red and purple bubble gum balls. To date, thank goodness, she only has one cavity.

Don't Miss Any of Nicki Holland's Exciting Adventures!

#1: The Case of the Mystery Mark

Strange things are happening at Pine Grove Middle School—vandalism, dog-napping, stolen papers and threatening notes. Is there a connection between the unusual new girl and the mysterious mark that keeps appearing whenever something goes wrong? Nicki and her best friends want to find out before something terrible happens to one of them!

#2: The Case of the Phantom Friend

Nicki and the girls have found a new friend in Lila Greaves. But someone has threatened Mrs. Greaves and now she could lose everything she loves. The girls have one clue that they hope will lead to something to save Mrs. Greaves—if only they can solve the mystery before it's too late!

#3: The Case of the Teenage Terminator

Christine's brother Tommy is in trouble, but he doesn't seem to realize it. Nicki, Meredith, Christine, Kim and Laura take on an investigation that pits them against a danger they've never faced before—one that could lead to a life-or-death struggle.

#4: The Case of the Terrified Track Star

Pine Grove's track star Jeremy Newkirk has always been afraid of dogs, but now somebody is using that information to scare him out of Saturday's important race. Without Jeremy, Pine Grove will never win! Following a trail of mysterious letters and threatening phone calls, Nicki and her friends are in their own

race against time to solve the mystery. Can the girls keep Jeremy's worst nightmare from coming true?

#5: The Case of the Counterfeit Cash

Nicki expected fun and sun in the summer before her eighth grade year—not mysterious strangers and counterfeit cash! Nicki, Meredith, Kim, Christine and Laura are warned to leave the mystery alone. But when Nicki is threatened, she has to solve the mystery to save her own life! (Coming March 1992.)

#6: The Case of the Haunting of Lowell Lanes

Nicki and her friends thought it would be fun to help Meredith's uncle at Lowell Lanes for the summer. But then the lights went out and strange things began to happen. Is Lowell Lanes really haunted? Can Nicki and her friends solve the mystery before Mr. Lowell is driven out of business? (Coming March 1992.)

Available at your local Christian bookstore.

Or have your parents call

Here's Life Publishers

1-800-950-4457

(Visa and Mastercard accepted.)